Carmen

and

The Venus of Ille

Prosper Mérimée

Translated by Andrew Brown

ALMA CLASSICS

ALMA CLASSICS
an imprint of

ALMA BOOKS LTD
Thornton House
Thornton Road
Wimbledon Village
London SW19 4NG
United Kingdom
www.almaclassics.com

Carmen first published in 1845; *The Venus of Ille* first published in 1834
These translations first published by Hesperus Press Ltd in 2004
These revised translations first published by Alma Classics in 2023
Translation, Introduction and Notes © Andrew Brown, 2023

Cover: Nathan Burton

Printed in Great Britain by CPI Group (UK) Ltd, Croydon CR0 4YY

MIX
Paper | Supporting
responsible forestry
FSC
www.fsc.org
FSC® C171272

ISBN: 978-1-84749-897-7

Contents

Introduction

The Prelude to Bizet's opera *Carmen* opens in an upbeat, some-what raucous A major, before swinging into an anticipation of the March of the Toreadors and then, after a sudden silence, modulating into the menacing D minor of the theme associated with the heroine, and with Fate. Soon we are in thrall to Carmen and her dark charms: the swaying hips, the rolling eyes, the assig-nations in the moonlit streets of Andalusia; a whiff of tobacco smoke, the swirl of the flounces and furbelows on a dress all scarlet and black, as she strikes a flamenco pose, head thrown back, leg extended, arm raised, castanets clacking, so come-hitherish and yet so disdainful; "*L'amour est enfant de bohème*", fortune-telling and smuggling, the almost liturgical murder of a woman outside the arena where, to the acclamations of the crowd, a bull is being ritually put to death...

The beginning of Mérimée's novella 'Carmen' strikes a rather different tone – indeed, in one sense, it is quite unreadable. If we don't understand ancient Greek, we won't know what the squiggly lines of the introductory quotation mean, since Mérimée – who later provides plenty of explanatory footnotes for the foreign languages in which his characters speak – here leaves us in the lurch. And if we *can* read the Greek, the epigram may well make us wince. It is a sourly misogynistic aperçu by the Alexandrian poet Palladas, and relies on a grim little pun as it informs us that there are only two occasions when a woman is any good: in bed (*en thalamo* – as in an "epithalamium") or dead (*en thanato*).

The Greeks had a word for it: woman is *cholos*, a source of bile or gall, something to make us angry (our word *choleric*). This is a querulous note to strike, and not to be excused by the plea that Palladas, a poverty-stricken schoolmaster and a diehard agnostic pagan in an age (the early fifth century) when Christianity seemed to be triumphing over the old gods across much of the Mediterranean world, appears to have been unhappily married. But Mérimée is not necessarily endorsing what he quotes. As they say these days, retweeting does not equate with agreement, and the novella that follows this laconic expression of bilious masculinity will hold up for inspection many attitudes and opinions from which it withholds any final assent. And Palladas's words serve the function of introducing us to the main themes, *thalamos* and *thanatos*, of Mérimée's story, which could also be called *A Song of Love and Death* – the title of Peter Conrad's study of opera, in which he often pairs Carmen with Don Giovanni as protagonists whose amoral freedom unto death (Carmen is "*liberté*", Don Giovanni sings "*Viva la libertà!*") in some sense figures the amorality of music itself.

Before we even meet Mérimée's two main characters, Don José and Carmen, we are introduced to the narrator, a somewhat dry, reflective figure who teasingly resembles Mérimée himself. Prosper Mérimée was a historian and antiquarian, an inspector of public monuments, and someone who did serious research for his fictional works. His *1572: A Chronicle of the Reign of Charles IX*, published in 1829, is unusually accurate for a historical novel, and he loved to haunt libraries, pore over manuscripts and indulge in archaeology both as a pastime and a profession – all passions that he shared with his friend Stendhal. It seems that 'Carmen' is based on a story Mérimée heard from the Countess de Montijo, mother of the French empress Eugénie (wife of Napoleon III). "It was all about that *jaque* [ruffian] from Málaga who had killed his mistress, who devoted herself exclusively to the public." The decision to make Carmen a *gitana* – something that has become part of her essence in the final story and most of the adaptations that have followed it – stemmed from the contingent fact that Mérimée just happened to have been studying *gitanos* for a while, and he liked to use what he knew. His interest in *gitanos* stemmed both from his travels in Spain and from an interest in Russian culture – he learnt the language, and, some time before embarking on 'Carmen', he read Pushkin's narrative poem *Tsygany* (*The Gypsies*), which he later translated into French prose. (Pushkin's poem has apparently inspired eighteen operas – even Shostakovich started to compose one.) It is symptomatic of this bookish man that, while serving a fortnight's jail sentence in Paris over a legal affair in which he took the "wrong" side, he whiled away the time brushing up his knowledge of Russian grammar.

Mérimée had a wide knowledge of Spain, and apparently spoke Spanish fluently, though one native speaker noted that his Spanish was a little archaic: he spoke the language of Don Quixote. Some of this knowledge, and in particular his understanding of the *gitano* way of life, was inevitably second-hand (borrowed… mainly from George Borrow). His narrator both evinces a certain familiarity with Spanish culture and casts doubt on the limits of his expertise. When we first meet him, he is wandering through the arid landscapes of Andalusia trying, text in hand, to identify the site of the Battle of Munda (45 BC). For all his dedication, it is with some relief that he comes across a patch of verdant grass, and surmises correctly that there is a watercourse nearby where he will find fresh water. A little later in the story, he spends his days researching in the library of the Dominicans in Córdoba; he passes his evenings sauntering along the River Guadalquivir with its bevy of local women bathing in the cooling streams. On these two occasions, relieved by the closeness of flowing waters, our Mr Dryasdust encounters, one after the other, the protagonists of the story he is telling us, Don José by the spring and Carmen by the river.

Not that the story simply sets up the narrator's French erudition, his claim to detached knowledge, as a contrast to the life and romance of the Spaniards, Basques, *gitanos* and others that he depicts. Rather, he shows how "knowledge" (or at least knowingness) and "life" are intertwined. He does his mansplaining with dry aplomb, and makes a parade of his learning, notably in the arch and mock-pompous little essay on the *gitanos* which he tagged on after the end of the story of 'Carmen' (not "mock" enough: this piece has dated badly). He indulges in cultural anthropology, or rather a knowing proneness to generalize. But the characters in his novella are *forced* to be *really* "knowing", to be everyday anthropologists, to observe the customs of the people among whom they live, as a matter of survival rather than as a scholarly pastime. Mérimée dabbles in amateur etymology; Carmen, like other *gitanos*, is – as the narrator acknowledges – an excellent linguist as a matter of life or death; her quickness of wit, her powers of mimicry, her *sharpness of tongue*, in every sense, leave Don José aghast and enthralled.

The narrator's observations about the people (and peoples) he is describing are tempered by a haze of scepticism about whether we can trust him. Carmen, like all outlaws – including eventually Don José – deceives to survive (and sometimes, in her case, just to have fun). Who can we trust in this tangled web of fictions? But in this story all the main characters are outsiders. The narrator is a Frenchman in Spain; Don José is a Basque; Carmen is a *gitana*, a nomad. The fractious love between the last two is the love between two people who are not at home. Don José is less at home with his homelessness than is Carmen. His nostalgia for his Basque homeland makes him fall a little too easily for Carmen's pretence (if it is pretence) that she is at least half Basque. But Carmen fiercely resists being tied down, by geography or law, or even love when it becomes too much of a bond, and she mocks him for docilely wanting to get back to barracks, or craving his homeland. When we first meet her, she immediately identifies herself as a *gitana* – but plays fast and loose with what that actually means. She is perfectly content to break the *gitano* code when it conflicts with what she wants, just as she will obey that code (with its subordination of a *romi*, a *gitana* wife, to her husband or *rom*) to its ultimate conclusion. She can adopt many disguises; she is capricious and shape-shifting; if she identifies herself as a *gitana*, for her that means identifying with non-identity – or, as she puts it, with freedom. Instead of the revolutionary motto "liberty or death", she seems to adopt the slogan "liberty *in* death". This casts a shadow (a "dark light", as the narrator puts it in another context, quoting Corneille) on our images of an absolute freedom that cannot – at least not in the terms of this novella – be fully realized. In any case, for Carmen, to do exactly as she pleases coexists with being bound to "superstitions", to the totems and taboos of her people. She is both id and, in her idiosyncratic way, identity. She is a unique, unpredictable, capricious force field *and* the essential, defiant *gitana*. All of this is summarized in what is almost her final, immensely complex taunting of Don José: "You're my *rom*, and as such you have the right to kill your *romi* – but Carmen will always be free."

'Carmen' tells many stories. *Carmen* is the Latin for song (and spell, or enchantment), and Mérimée's prose has its own polyphonic music, a little drier than the gorgeous swagger and doom-laden vibrato of Bizet's opera, but just as bewitching. These stories include the following. There is a narrator who is drawn to a foreign country (and that other foreign country, the past) that he cannot quite grasp (where on earth was the Battle of Munda fought?). There is a member of a minority (the Basque Don José) who falls in love with a member of another minority (the *gitana* Carmen). There is the jealous, possessive man who kills a woman because she rejects him. There is the same man who, by murdering his unattainable beloved, seems to know, or at least eventually accepts, that this will mean his own death. There is a woman who claims to be *beyond identity* (radically free) and who yet remains defiantly loyal to her identity as a *gitana*. This in turn, for a reader nowadays, cannot fail to evoke the fate of the wider categories, the long-term histories, to which she belongs. She is a woman killed by male violence. She is a *gitana* murdered by a non-*gitano*. In the essay that follows his story, Mérimée uses the word "gentile" to refer to non-*gitanos*: on first meeting

Carmen, the narrator wonders whether she might be Moorish or (and here he hesitates) Jewish. One of the multiple stories that the text points to is that of Spain itself, with its plural histories. This is a culture that, at certain moments, has been obsessed with *limpieza de sangre*, or "purity of blood" (that is, being a Roman Catholic with no admixture of Muslim or Jewish identity) – and yet one of the key signifiers of Hispanicity, the word "*Olé!*", has a (perhaps deceptive) resemblance to "Allah!"; the Grand Inquisitor Torquemada may well have had *converso* ancestry; and the grandfather of St Teresa of Ávila, patroness of Spain, was himself, it seems, a Jewish *converso*. Carmen, who so often makes us think of Spain, is an outsider in a country of outsiders – though some outsiders, of course, are more outside than others.

Mérimée's story begins with the narrator embarking on a quest for the long-lost battleground of Munda, which ended the Civil War between Caesar and Pompey. Does he eventually locate it? For all the fascination of ancient history, the point is surely that Spain (and the modern world in general) is still the site of far from mundane battles in a civil (or uncivil) war that has not come to an end, a war in which rival factions, split by gender, ethnicity, religion, class, sexuality and many other badges of identity – all of which are brandished or alluded to in 'Carmen' – continue to confront one another.

'The Venus of Ille', like 'Carmen', is a story about a fateful female told by a bookish, somewhat aloof male figure similar to Mérimée. Again, the narrator is far from home, in France's deep south, with its provincial ways and its folklore, as much Catalan as French. Again the tale is propped up by an anthropological-philological apparatus, based as it is on the unearthing of a sinister bronze statue, black in colour (just as Carmen is "black", since this is how *gitanos* in that story often identify themselves). Like 'Carmen' it begins with a Greek epigraph and is likewise a product of Mérimée's career in the heritage industry: he had, for instance, visited the monastery of Serrabone (close to the town of Ille, and referred to in the story) in his capacity as Inspector General of Historic Monuments.

Like 'Carmen', it is also a story about the fraught, tragicomical passage from one language to another. The polyglot Carmen is able to dupe the English lord with her deliberate mistranslation of the word *maquila*; old Peyrehorade, the amateur epigrapher in 'The Venus of Ille', says, mock-modestly, "Perhaps you'll laugh at my translation" of the inscriptions on the statue of Venus. But the misfit of languages and cultures, yet again, is no laughing matter. The amiable if fatuous Peyrehorade and his family meet with a terrible punishment. Who exacts this punishment, and why, is never entirely clear. Is it a humiliated visitor from Spain getting his own back for his drubbing in a game of pelota? Or is the statue of Venus, which the bridegroom Alphonse de Peyrehorade and other locals treat with a degree of over-familiarity or even aggression, involved? And while Venus is indeed dishonoured in the course of the story, the sinister smile on her statue's face has been there right from the start, suggesting that she was already prone to malice when the piece was first cast centuries ago. Maybe the "blasphemy" is carried out against true love in the form of the self-seeking and self-satisfied Alphonse's arranged and meretricious marriage, which the narrator grumbles against. A Freudian might see Venus's revenge as the return of the repressed: a libido that has been sacrificed to lucre here displays its power in a violent epiphany similar to that meted out by blasphemed deities in the plays of Euripides. Not for nothing does Mérimée's story keep harking back, with apparent light-heartedness but in fact dreadful appropriateness, to classical precedents such as Racine's *Phèdre*, itself a version of Euripides's *Hippolytus*, in which a rejected Aphrodite wreaks havoc.

The lack of any persuasive "naturalistic" explanation for the murder of Peyrehorade suggests that the author is writing something that is as close to the numinous and at times eerie world of

Greek and Roman myth as it is to nineteenth-century France. The teasing aspects of the story – the satire on amateur etymologists and pompous antiquarians, including the ironic depiction of the pedantic narrator – in no way undermines the story's haunting effectiveness. The Venus figure has particular resonance today. It is not just a pagan deity, or, allegorically, some ideal of true love or some fundamental instinctual drive (such as the libido) that is being mocked and that takes revenge. It is, more specifically, a *statue*. Statues these days are forever being toppled: Marxes, Lenins and Stalins are consigned to the rubbish heap of history, Buddhas are dynamited (and not just because "all compound things are subject to decay"), the slave trader Edward Coulston is thrown into the harbour, "Rhodes Must Fall". But a statue is the closest thing in classical art to a realistic depiction of the human body. That is why a statue can be so uncanny, and why the iconoclasm that indulges in the destruction of "idols", however necessary it may be (the Second Commandment), is a serious business. In Mérimée's story, the statue is not destroyed – at least not initially – but simply turned into a prop in a piece of tomfoolery. But this little joke ends up having the symbolic gravity, and the fateful consequences, of Don Giovanni inviting the statue of the Commendatore to supper. And the trope of the statue coming alive – if this is what happens – and the work of art that is more powerful than its creators and contemplators, fits into a set of archetypal desires and anxieties that stretch forward to today's world of robots and artificial intelligence.

As we have seen, Mérimée was prone to including jocular references to the limits of his (and anybody's) knowledge. He loved literary hoaxes – what the French call "mystifications"; his career as a writer began with a volume of plays purporting to have been written by the fictitious Spanish actress Clara Gazul and translated into French by the non-existent Joseph L'Estrange. 'Carmen' and 'The Venus of Ille' are in certain ways *mystifications*, and their matter-of-fact dryness of language conceals several puns, private jokes and bits of cod scholarship that anticipate Nabokov (whose *Lolita* is haunted by the image of the heroine as an underage Carmen). But mystification in no way undermines a sense of mystery – and when riddling philology tangles with embodied passions, the result is often tragedy.

Carmen and After

'Carmen' is dangerous. Mérimée's novella puts a finger on so many of the sore points of modern life that it should come with a health warning ("includes ethnic stereotypes, violence, language, scenes of smoking"). *Plus ça change*: when the story was first published in 1845, in the *Revue des Deux Mondes*, many scandalized readers cancelled their subscriptions.

It is not only Carmen who stands at an angle to any questions of identity. The ethnic group to which she belongs has many names. Where Mérimée writes "*bohémien*", in Spanish contexts I have generally used the Spanish word *gitano* with the relevant ending. The word *gitano* gives us access to the "Egyptian" business undertaken by Carmen and her colleagues; it also sounds (to English ears) foreign, just as *bohémien* draws on the idea that the ethnic group in question came from Bohemia. Where the context is more broadly European, I have used the word "Roma". Some Roma these days are justifiably wary of self-identification, hence their absence from censuses and tables of statistics. Others are proud to identify as Roma, or use some other term. The Rom, the Dom, the Lom are all ethnic labels that seem to allude to a "non-dom", nomadic ontology. There is an interesting discussion of this in an essay by Gregor Dufunia Kwiek in *All Change! Romani Studies through Romani Eyes*, edited by Damian Le Bas and Thomas Acton (Hatfield: University of Hertfordshire Press, 2010), a volume of essays in which the culturally anthropologized become their own cultural anthropologists: Kwiek's article has the wonderful title 'Afterword: Rom, Roma, Romani, Kale, Gypsies, Travellers and Sinti… Pick a Name and Stick with It, Already!' (pp. 79–83), an injunction with which it is (fortunately) impossible to comply. The interested reader is referred to 'Tackling Inequalities Faced by Gypsy, Roma and Traveller Communities', a House of Commons Committee Report (Seventh Report of Session 2017–19), which is available online.

The symbolic richness of Mérimée's economically told novella has led to many later homages, adaptations, reworkings and subversions, many of them mediated by Bizet's opera. *Carmen* seems to have been idolized by men of a philological cast of mind, such as Nietzsche and Joyce. Nietzsche, who admired dryness, rated Mérimée as a "master of prose". He loved Bizet's opera, finding its "cheerfulness" to be "African": "fate hangs over it, its happiness is short, sudden, unforgiving. […] How much good we derive from the yellow afternoons of its happiness!" The love it depicts is "fate, fatality, *fatefulness*; cynical, innocent, cruel – and for that very reason part of *nature*!" Perhaps Nietzsche is out to promote Carmen as a specifically Nietzschean *femme fatale*, a heroine "beyond good and evil". He is also intent on setting Bizet up as the antidote to Wagner, from whose influence he spent the last part of his life trying to escape (the preceding quotation is from the beginning of his book *The Case of Wagner: A Musician's Problem*). It is amusing to read that Bizet's *Carmen* was initially condemned for being "too Wagnerian", and touching to note that Wagner apparently praised Bizet's opera. As for Joyce, in *Ulysses*, with its many jocular references to opera (see Lenehan), Molly Bloom – with her Gibraltarian antecedents – is a Dublin Carmen, fortunately with a resigned and semi-*complaisant* Poldy as husband rather than a despairing Don José.

There have been many cinematic adaptations of 'Carmen', usually based more on the opera than on Mérimée's story, and involving greater or lesser degrees of flamenco: two came out in 1983 – Carlos Saura's is a dance-based spectacle, Peter Brook's is a dark and concentrated chamber opera. Earlier, Otto Preminger had created *Carmen Jones* (1954), with an all-black cast; 2001 saw *Carmen: A Hip Hopera*, which also gives the story an African American spin, with Beyoncé starring as Carmen Brown. Directed by Robert Townsend, it steers away from relying on Bizet's music, as does Jean-Luc Godard in his *Prénom Carmen* ("First Name: Carmen", 1984): Godard's film has a few people whistling or humming bits of Bizet, but its soundtrack mainly deploys late Beethoven quartets (as well as the waves of the sea). Godard's Carmen introduces herself in a voice-over as "the girl who should not be called Carmen", and Carmen can stray very far from her original identity while still retaining the power of Mérimée's *gitana* to shock and inspire. All of these versions are powerful and convincing recreations: they indulge, often inventively, in a "stereotyping" and "cultural appropriation" which they simultaneously question. Carmen will doubtless continue to be reincarnated on the screen, in a variety of geographical and cultural settings: a version directed by Benjamin Millepied, due for general release in the spring of 2023, apparently has a cast that includes the doyenne of Pedro Almodóvar films, Rossy de Palma, and moves from Mexico to Los Angeles.

Like so many other countries, the land of Mérimée and Bizet has not always cared to have too many Carmens on its territory. In 2009–10, in violation of EU laws, the French government expelled over eleven thousand Roma to their "countries of origin".

Further Reading

Charnon-Deutsch, Lou, *The Spanish Gypsy: The History of a European Obsession* (University Park: Penn State University Press, 2004)

Cortés, Ismael and Fernández, Cayetano, 'Long Sad History of Roma in Spain', in *Le Monde diplomatique*, May 2015

Johnson, Jeremy, 'Considering Carmen: Great Art, Harmful Stereotypes and a 21st-Century Dilemma', article on houston-grandopera.org

Northup, George T., 'The Influence of George Borrow on Prosper Mérimée', *Modern Philology*, Vol. 13, No. 3 (July 1915), pp. 143–56

Cañadas Ortega, Araceli, 'Anti-Gypsy Legislation in Spain from the Catholic Kings to the Great Raid', article on romarchive.eu

Tsou, Judy, 'Cultural Contrast in Bizet's *Carmen* at the Opéra Comique', article on seattleoperablog.com

This translation is dedicated
to the memory of my father, with my love.

– Andrew Brown, 2023

CARMEN

Πᾶσα γυνὴ χόλος ἐστίν· ἔχει δ᾽ ἀγαθὰς δύο ὥρας,
τὴν μίαν ἐν θαλάμῳ, τὴν μίαν ἐν θανάτῳ

PALLADAS*

I

I had always suspected that the geographers had no idea what they were talking about when they situated the Battle of Munda in the territory of the Bastuli-Poeni, near present-day Monda, some two leagues or so north of Marbella. My own conjectures, based on the anonymous text known as the *Bellum Hispaniense*, and some information I gleaned in the Duke of Osuna's well-stocked library, led me to think that the Montilla area was a better place to look for the memorable site where, for the last time, Caesar played double or quits against the champions of the Republic. I happened to be in Andalusia at the beginning of autumn 1830, and I made an excursion sufficiently extensive to clear up my remaining doubts. A paper that I intend to publish soon will, I hope, leave no trace of uncertainty in the minds of all true archaeologists.* While I wait for my thesis to resolve, once and for all, the geographical problem that is keeping all the scholars of Europe in suspense, I want to tell you a little story; it will in no way prejudice the fascinating question of the true site of Munda.

I had hired a guide and two horses in Córdoba, and sallied forth with Caesar's *Commentaries** and a few shirts as my only luggage. One day, wandering across the high ground of the Carchena plain,* overwhelmed by exhaustion, dying of thirst and roasted by a scorching sun, I was quite sincerely wishing that Caesar

3

and the sons of Pompey would all go to hell, when, at some distance from the path I was following, I caught sight of a small stretch of green grass interspersed with rushes and reeds. From this I guessed that there must be a spring nearby. And indeed, when I went over to it, I saw that what I had taken for a grassy lawn was in fact a bog into which vanished a stream apparently flowing from a narrow gorge between two high foothills of the Sierra de Cabra. I deduced that if I made my way upstream I would find fresher water, fewer leeches and frogs, and perhaps a little shade amidst the rocks. At the mouth of the gorge, my horse whinnied, and another horse that I couldn't see immediately replied. I had hardly gone a hundred paces or so before the gorge suddenly widened out onto a kind of natural semicircular arena perfectly well shaded by the height of the surrounding escarpments. It would have been impossible to stumble across anywhere that promised the traveller a more pleasant place to rest. At the foot of the sheer cliffs, the stream shot out, bubbling and foaming, to fall into a small pool lined with snowy-white sand. Five or six fine, verdant oak trees, permanently sheltered from the wind and watered by the cool spring, rose at its edges, and covered it with their thick, leafy shade – and, to complete the picture, the slender lustrous grass surrounding the pool offered a better bed than you could have found in any hostelry for ten leagues around.

It was not to me that fell the honour of having discovered such a lovely spot. There was already a man resting there, probably asleep, when I came across it. Woken up by the whinnying, he had risen to his feet and gone over to his horse, which had been taking advantage of its master's sleep to feast on the nearby grass. He was a strapping young fellow, of middling height but robust appearance, with proud and sombre eyes. His complexion, which might once have been handsome, had become, thanks to the sun, darker than his hair. In one hand he held his horse's halter, in the other a brass blunderbuss. I have to admit that, at first, the blunderbuss and the fierce expression of the man bearing it made me slightly apprehensive – but I'd stopped believing in thieves, since I'd heard so much about them and yet never met a single one. In any case, I'd seen so many honest farmers arming themselves to the teeth to go to market that the sight of a firearm didn't give me any cause to doubt the stranger's honesty.

"And then," I said to myself, "what would he do with my shirts and my Elzevir edition of the *Commentaries*?"*

So I gave the man with the blunderbuss a friendly nod and asked, with a smile, whether I had disturbed his sleep. Without answering, he looked me over from head to toe – then, as if satisfied by his examination, he turned the same attentive gaze on my guide, who was coming up behind me. I saw the latter grow pale and halt, showing signs of evident terror.

"Maybe a hold-up!" I said to myself.

But I immediately decided to do the sensible thing and not show the least sign of anxiety. I dismounted; I told the guide to unbridle the horse, and, kneeling down at the edge of the spring, I thrust my head and my hands into the water, then I drank a good mouthful of it, lying on my stomach, like Gideon's bad soldiers.*

Meanwhile, I observed both my guide and the stranger. The former came over to me, albeit with great reluctance; the latter didn't seem to be harbouring any hostile intentions against us, since he'd left his horse free to roam, and his blunderbuss – which at first he'd levelled horizontally at us – was now drooping earthwards.

Thinking I ought not to take offence at his apparent lack of respect for my person, I stretched out on the grass and casually asked the man with the blunderbuss if he had flint and steel on him. As I spoke, I took out my cigar case. The stranger, still without a word, dug into his pocket, pulled out his lighter and swiftly lit my cigar. Evidently he was now starting to show a more human side – he sat down opposite me, though he didn't lay his weapon down. Once my cigar was alight, I chose the best of the ones remaining, and asked him if he smoked.

"Yes, sir," he replied. These were the first words he had uttered, and I noticed that he didn't pronounce his *s* in the Andalusian style,* which led me to conclude that he was a traveller like me, only less of an archaeologist.

"You'll find this one's pretty good," I told him, presenting him with a real Havana regalia.*

He bowed his head slightly, lit his cigar from mine, thanked me with another nod, then started to smoke, with all the appearance of intense enjoyment.

"Ah!" he exclaimed, slowly exhaling his first puff through his mouth and nostrils. "It's been such a long time since I had a smoke!"

In Spain, a cigar offered and accepted establishes relations of hospitality, as does sharing bread and salt in the Orient. My new acquaintance turned out to be chattier than I'd expected. Furthermore, although he claimed he lived in the *partido* of Montilla,* he seemed not to be very familiar with this particular area. He didn't know the name of the delightful valley we were in – he couldn't identify any of the villages nearby – and when I asked him whether he had perhaps seen any ruined walls, big tiles with broad rims* or stone carvings, he confessed that he'd never paid much attention to such things. On the other hand, he did demonstrate his expertise on the subject of horses. He criticized mine, which wasn't difficult – then he gave me the pedigree of his own, a product of the famous Córdoba stud farm: this was indeed a noble beast, so untiringly energetic, his master claimed, that on one occasion he'd done thirty leagues in a single day,* at full gallop or at a brisk trot. In the middle of his monologue, the stranger abruptly stopped, as if surprised and vexed at himself for having said too much.

"The reason was, I was in a real hurry to get to Córdoba," he continued, looking slightly embarrassed. "I had to go and canvass the judges about a trial…" As he spoke, he fixed his eyes on my guide Antonio, who lowered his eyes.

The shade and the stream put me in such a good mood that I remembered a few slices of excellent ham that my friends from Montilla had put in my guide's saddlebag. I had them brought over, and I invited the stranger to take his portion of the improvised meal. If it had been a long time since he had smoked, it seemed more than probable to me that he hadn't eaten for at least forty-eight hours. He devoured the food like a starving wolf. I guessed that meeting me had been a stroke of good fortune for the poor devil. My guide, however, ate little, drank even less and spoke not at all, despite the fact that since the beginning of our journey he had shown himself to be an unstoppable chatterbox. The presence of our guest seemed to bother him, and a certain mistrust kept them apart from one another without my being able to divine any definite cause.

The last morsels of bread and ham had already disappeared; we had each smoked a second cigar; I ordered the guide to bridle our horses, and I was just about to take my leave of my new friend when he asked me where I intended to spend the night.

Before I could notice my guide signalling to me, I had replied that I was going to the Venta del Cuervo.*

"A bad lodging for a person such as yourself, sir… I'm going there too, and, if you'll allow me to keep you company, we can make our way there together."

"With great pleasure," I said, climbing onto my horse.

My guide, who was holding my stirrup for me, again caught my eye as he pulled a dubious face. I responded with a shrug, as if to reassure him that I was perfectly easy in my own mind – and off we set.

Antonio's mysterious gestures, his anxiety, the few words the stranger had let drop – above all, his thirty-league dash and the rather implausible explanation he had given for it – had already enabled me to form an opinion of my travelling companion. I had no doubt that the man with me was a smuggler, perhaps a thief – but so what? I knew the Spanish character well enough to be completely sure I had nothing to fear from a man who had eaten and smoked with me. His very presence was a reliable protection against us encountering any mishap. In any case, I was not at all displeased to come across a real bandit. It's not every day that you meet such a man, and there's a certain charm in finding yourself next to a dangerous character, especially when you sense that he's really quite tame and gentle.

I hoped by degrees to bring the stranger round to confiding in me, and, despite my guide's winks and headshakes, I brought the conversation round to the topic of highway robbers. Of course, I spoke of them with great respect. There was at that time in Andalusia a notorious bandit called José María,* whose exploits were on everyone's lips.

"What if I were riding next to José María?..." I said to myself.

I related the stories I knew about that hero, all of which redounded to his honour, of course, and I ringingly expressed my deep admiration for his bravery and his nobility.

"José María is nothing but a rascal," the stranger said coldly.

"Is he merely doing himself justice, or is it an excess of modesty on his part?" I asked myself – for, by dint of thinking long and hard about my companion, I had ended up applying to him the description of José María that I had seen on the posters set up at the gates of many a town in Andalusia. "Yes, it must be him... Blond hair, blue eyes, wide mouth, fine teeth, a velvet jacket with silver buttons, white skin leggings, a bay horse... No doubt about it! But let's respect his incognito."*

We arrived at the *venta*. It was just as he'd made it out to be – one of the most wretched that I'd yet encountered. One big room served as kitchen, dining room and bedroom. There was a fire burning on a flat stone in the middle of the room, and the smoke curled up through a hole in the roof, or rather gathered there, forming a cloud a few feet above the ground. All along the foot of the wall you could see five or six old mule blankets laid out – the travellers' beds. Twenty or so yards from the house, or rather from the single room I have just described, there rose a kind of shed serving as a stable. In this delightful hostelry there were no other human beings – at least at that particular moment – apart from an old woman and a little girl between ten and twelve years old, both of them sooty in hue and dressed in dreadful rags.

"So this is all that remains," I said to myself, "of the populace of ancient Munda Baetica!* O Caesar! O Sextus Pompeius! How surprised you would be if you were to return to this world!"

When she noticed my companion, the old woman uttered an involuntary exclamation of surprise.

"Ah! My lord Don José!" she exclaimed.

Don José scowled, and raised his hand in a gesture of authority that immediately made the old woman fall silent. I turned to my guide, and, with a barely perceptible sign, intimated that there was nothing he could tell me about the man with whom I was going to spend the night that I didn't already know. The supper was better than I'd expected. On a small table just a foot high, we were served with an old fricasseed cockerel with rice and plenty of hot pepper, then peppers in oil, and finally gazpacho, a kind of salad with peppers.* Three such spicy dishes obliged us to have frequent recourse to a wineskin full of Montilla,* which turned out to be delicious. When I'd finished eating, I spotted a mandolin hanging on the wall – there are mandolins everywhere in Spain – and I asked the little girl serving us if she could play.

"No," she replied, "but Don José plays really well!"

"Perhaps you'd be kind enough," I asked him, "to sing me something – I'm passionately fond of your national music."

9

"I cannot refuse anything to such a decent gentleman who gives me such excellent cigars," exclaimed Don José good-humouredly – and, asking for the mandolin to be reached over to him, he started to sing while playing at the same time. His voice was rough and yet pleasant, and the melody was melancholy and bizarre. As for the words, I couldn't understand a single one.

"Unless I'm mistaken," I said to him, "it's not a Spanish melody you've just been singing. It resembles the *zorzicos** I've heard in the Provinces,* and the words must be in Basque."

"Yes," replied Don José, with a sombre expression.

He set the mandolin down on the ground and, folding his arms, started to gaze at the waning fire, looking strangely melancholy. Lit up by a lamp placed on the little table, his face, at once noble and wild, reminded me of Milton's Satan. Like him, perhaps, my companion was dreaming of the home he had left, of the exile he had incurred through some misdeed. I tried to rekindle the conversation, but he didn't reply, absorbed as he was in his own gloomy thoughts. The old woman had already gone to bed in a corner of the room, behind a blanket full of holes stretched out on a piece of rope. The little girl had followed her into this retreat reserved for the fair sex. Then my guide, rising to his feet, invited me to follow him to the stable – but at his words Don José, as if waking up with a start, asked him brusquely where he was going.

"To the stable," answered the guide.

"What're you going there for? The horses have enough food. Sleep here – your master will let you."

"I'm afraid my master's horse may be ill. I'd like him to have a look – perhaps he'll know what needs to be done."

It was obvious that Antonio wanted to speak to me in private, but I was anxious not to arouse Don José's suspicions, and, given the way things now stood between us, I felt the best I could do was put on a show of complete trust. So I replied to Antonio that I didn't know a thing about horses, and wanted to get some sleep.

Don José followed him to the stable, and soon returned alone. He told me there was nothing wrong with the horse, but my guide considered him such a precious animal that he was giving him a rub-down with his jacket to make him sweat, and clearly intended to spend the whole night engaged in this pleasant task. Meanwhile, I had stretched out on the mule blankets, wrapping myself carefully in my cloak so as not to touch them. After begging my pardon for the liberty he was taking in passing the night with me, Don José lay down in front of the door, not before priming his blunderbuss afresh and carefully placing it under the saddlebag he used as a pillow. Five minutes after we had wished each other goodnight, we were both fast asleep.

I'd thought I was tired enough to be able to sleep in such a lodging, but, after an hour, some really unpleasant itching sensations forced me out of my first slumbers. As soon as I realized what was causing them, I got up, convinced that it would be better to spend the rest of the night out in the open rather than under this inhospitable roof. Walking on tiptoe, I reached the door and stepped over the recumbent form of Don José, who was sleeping the sleep of the just, and I managed to step outside without him waking up. Near the door there was a wide wooden bench: I stretched out on it and made myself as comfortable as I could for the rest of the night. I was just about to close my eyes for the second time when I dimly saw the shadows of a man and a horse passing in front of me, both of them walking along without making the slightest noise. I sat up, and thought I recognized Antonio. Surprised to see him outside the stable at this hour of the night, I got up and walked over to him. He had already halted on seeing me.

"Where is he?" Antonio asked in a low voice.

"In the *venta*. He's asleep – he's not afraid of the bugs. So why are you taking this horse away?"

I noticed at this point that, so as not to make any noise as he left the shed, Antonio had carefully wrapped the animal's hooves in the tatters of an old blanket.

"Don't talk so loud," said Antonio, "for God's sake! You don't know who that man is. He's José Navarro, the most notorious bandit in Andalusia. All day long I've been making signs to you, and you just wouldn't get the message."

"Bandit or not, what's it matter to me?" I replied. "He hasn't robbed us, and I'd bet he doesn't have any intention of doing so."

"Sure, but there are two hundred ducats' reward for anyone who hands him in. I know of a lancers' post a league and a half from here, and before daylight I'm going to bring a few strong sturdy lads back with me. I'd have taken his horse, but the beast's so fierce that only old Navarro can get anywhere near it."

"Devil take you!" I said. "What wrong has the poor man done to you for you to turn him in? Anyway, are you sure he's the bandit you say he is?"

"Absolutely sure: just now he followed me into the stable and said, 'You look like you know me. If you tell that gentleman who I am, I'll blow your brains out.' Go on, sir: just you stay with him – you have nothing to fear. As long as he knows you're there, he won't suspect a thing."

As we talked, we'd already gone far enough from the *venta* for the horse's hooves not to be audible. In the twinkling of an eye, Antonio had stripped its hooves of the rags he'd wrapped them in; he was preparing to straddle his mount. I tried to hold him back with pleas and menaces.

"I'm a poor devil, sir," he kept saying. "Two hundred ducats aren't to be sneezed at, especially when you can free the country from vermin like that at the same time. But take care: if old Navarro wakes up, he'll whip out his blunderbuss, and then look out! I've gone too far to pull back now, but you sort things out the best you can."

The rascal was already in the saddle; he spurred on his horse, and in the darkness I had soon lost sight of him.

I was more than irritated at my guide, and really rather worried. After a moment's reflection, I made my mind up and went back into the *venta*. Don José was still asleep, doubtless making up at that moment for the exertions and lack of sleep he had endured for several adventure-filled days. I was obliged to shake him roughly to wake him up. I'll never forget the fierce expression in his eyes and the movement he made to seize his blunderbuss – which, as a precautionary measure, I had moved some distance away from where he lay.

"Sir," I said, "I beg your pardon for waking you, but I have a rather silly question to ask you: would you like to see half a dozen lancers turning up here?"

He jumped to his feet, and asked me in a terrible voice, "Who told you that?"

"It hardly matters where I got the information, so long as it's accurate."

"Your guide has betrayed me – but he'll pay for it! Where is he?"

"I don't know… In the stable, I think… but someone has told me…"

"Who told you?… It can't be the old woman…"

"Someone I don't know… Let's cut the chatter: do you have, yes or no, any reasons not to hang about waiting for soldiers? If you do, don't waste any more time, otherwise goodnight, and I'm sorry for interrupting your sleep."

"Ah! Your guide! Your guide! I'd been suspicious of him right from the start… but… well, now he's done for!… Goodbye, sir. May God return the good deed I owe you. I'm not altogether as bad as you think me… yes, there's something about me that deserves the pity of a gentleman like you… Goodbye, sir… I have just one regret: that I can't repay my debt to you."

"In return for the service I have rendered you, promise me, Don José, not to suspect anyone, not to think of vengeance. Look, here are some cigars for the road – bon voyage!" And I held out my hand to him.

He shook it without replying, picked up his blunderbuss and his saddlebag and, after saying a few words to the old woman in a language I couldn't understand, he rushed to the shed. A few moments later, I heard him galloping across the countryside.

For my part, I lay down on my bench again, but I didn't get back to sleep. I kept wondering if I'd been right to save a thief, and perhaps a murderer, from the gallows for the sole reason that I'd eaten ham with him and rice done Valencian-style. Hadn't I betrayed my guide, who was upholding the law? Hadn't I exposed him to the vengeance of a wicked man? But what about the laws of hospitality?... The prejudice of a savage, I told myself – I'll have to answer for all the crimes which that bandit will commit... But is it really such a prejudice, this instinctive conscience that resists all our powers of reasoning? Perhaps, in the delicate situation in which I found myself, I was going to feel remorse whatever decision I made.

I was still dithering, in the greatest uncertainty as to the rightness of my action, when I saw half a dozen horsemen appearing with Antonio, who was prudently bringing up the rear. I went to meet them, and informed them that the bandit had taken flight over two hours ago. The old woman, when questioned by the corporal, replied that she knew old Navarro, but, as she lived all alone, she would never have dared to risk her life by denouncing him. She added that, whenever he came to her place, it was his habit always to leave in the middle of the night. As for me, I was obliged to go to a place a few leagues away so they could inspect my passport and sign a declaration in the presence of an *alcalde*,* after which I was allowed to continue with my archaeological research. Antonio bore me a grudge, suspecting that I was the one who'd prevented him from getting his two hundred ducats. Still, when we reached Córdoba, we separated as good friends. I gave him as big a tip as the state of my finances would allow...

II

I spent a few days in Córdoba. I'd been given details of a certain manuscript in the library of the Dominicans, where I would find some interesting information about ancient Munda. I was given a warm welcome by the good Fathers, and spent my days in their monastery, while in the evenings I would go for a stroll through the town. At Córdoba, towards sunset, you always find several loiterers on the quayside that runs along the right bank of the Guadalquivir. Here you have to endure the stench from a tannery that still maintains the region's ancient renown for the preparation of leather, but on the other hand, this means you can enjoy a sight that brings its own rewards. A few minutes before the angelus, a good number of women gather by the riverside, at the foot of the quay, whose wall rises quite high. No man would dare to mingle with this troop. As soon as the angelus sounds, it's deemed to be night-time. At the last chime of the bell, all these women take off their clothes and get into the water – and then there's a real outburst of shouting and laughter, a hellish din. From up on the quay, men gaze down at the bathing beauties, straining their eyes but still not able to make out much of their shapes. And yet those vague white outlines, on the dark blue of the river, stir poetically inclined minds, and, with a little imagination, it isn't difficult to dream that you can see Diana and her nymphs bathing, though you need not fear the fate of Actaeon.* I've heard that, one day, some young brats clubbed together to grease the palm of the cathedral bell-ringer and get him to ring the angelus twenty minutes before the legitimate time. Although it was still broad daylight, the nymphs of the Guadalquivir did not hesitate, and, placing their trust in the angelus rather than the sun, they took their bath – which is always the plainest and simplest affair imaginable – in all good conscience. I wasn't there. In my time, the bell-ringer was incorruptible, the twilight rather dim, and it would have needed a cat to distinguish the oldest orange seller from the prettiest young *grisette* in Córdoba.*

One evening, at the hour when you can no longer see a thing, I was having a smoke, leaning on the parapet of the quay, when a woman, climbing up the steps that lead down to the river, came and sat next to me. In her hair she was wearing a big spray of jasmine, which in the evenings gives off an intoxicating perfume. She was simply – perhaps even poorly – dressed, all in black, like most young working-class women in the evenings. Fashionable women wear black only in the mornings; in the evenings, they dress *a la francesa*.* As she came near me, my bather let the mantilla covering her head slip down over her shoulders, and, *in the dark light that falls from the stars*,* I saw that she was young and petite, with a nice figure, and that she had very big eyes. I immediately threw away my cigar. She understood the meaning of this attentive, French-style politeness, and hastened to tell me that she was very fond of the smell of tobacco, and indeed that she herself sometimes smoked, when she could find some mild *papelitos*.* As luck would have it, I had some in my cigar case, and I quickly offered her one. She condescended to take one, and lit it from a bit of burning rope that a child brought us for a penny. Mingling the smoke of our tobacco, we chatted for so long, the lovely bather and myself, that we found ourselves almost alone on the quay. I didn't think it indiscreet to propose that we go and have an ice cream at the *nevería*.* After a modest hesitation, she accepted, but before she finally agreed, she wanted to know what time it was. I wound up my watch to make it chime, and the noise seemed to give her great cause for astonishment.

"Ah, you foreigners! What inventions people have come up with in your countries! What part of the world are you from, sir? You're English, I imagine?"*

"French, in fact, and your humble servant. And you, miss, or madam, you must be from Córdoba?"

"No."

"You're Andalusian, at least. I think I can recognize this from your soft accent."

"If you're so good at spotting people's accents, you must be able to guess who I am."

"I think you're from the land of Jesus, a mere skip and a jump from paradise."

(I had learnt this metaphor, which designates Andalusia, from my friend Francisco Sevilla, the well-known picador.)*

"Paradise – pah!… People round here say that paradise isn't meant for the likes of us."

"In that case you could be Moorish, or…" I stopped, not daring to say "Jewish".

"Oh, come off it! You can see perfectly well that I'm a *gitana* – would you like me to tell your *baji*?* Have you heard of la Carmencita? That's me."

I was such an unbeliever, fifteen years ago, that I didn't even recoil in horror on finding myself sitting right next to a witch.

"Well!" I said to myself. "Last week I had supper with a highway robber – now look at me, having an ice cream with a servant of the Devil. Ah well… when in Rome…"

I had yet another reason to cultivate her acquaintance. On leaving school, I must confess to my shame, I'd wasted a fair bit of time studying the occult sciences, and had even, on several occasions, tried to summon up the Spirit of Darkness. Although I had long been cured of the passion for such investigations, all superstitions still held a certain allure for my curious mind, and I was really looking forward to learning the heights attained by the art of magic among *gitanos*.

While we were chatting, we had entered the *nevería*, and sat down at a little table lit by a candle enclosed in a round glass vessel. So I had plenty of time to examine my *gitana*, while several respectable folk there paused over their ices, astounded to see me in such good company.

I really doubt whether Miss Carmen was of pure race – at least, she was infinitely prettier than all the women of her nation that I've ever met. For a woman to be beautiful, she must, the Spanish say, combine thirty lots of *si** – or, if you prefer, you must be able to define her by ten adjectives that are each applicable to three parts of her person. For example, she must have three black things: her eyes, her eyelids and her eyebrows; three slender things: her fingers, her lips and her hair; etc. See Brantôme for the rest.* My *gitana* could not lay claim to so many perfections. Her skin, which was completely even-toned, was almost copper-hued. Her eyes were slanting, but admirably wide; her lips were a bit prominent, but nicely shaped, showing teeth whiter than blanched almonds. Her hair, perhaps a little on the thick side, was black, with a bluish gleam like a crow's wing, long and glossy. To avoid wearying you with an over-prolix description, I'll simply tell you, in short, that she made up for every defect with some good point, which perhaps stood out all the more strongly in contrast. Hers was a strange and savage beauty – a face which at first made you stand and stare, but one that you couldn't forget. Her eyes, especially, had an expression at once voluptuous and untamed that I have never since found in any human being. "*Gitano*'s eye, wolf's eye" – a Spanish saying that is applied to anyone with acute powers of observation. If you don't have time to go to the zoo to study the gaze of a wolf, just look at your cat when it's about to pounce on a sparrow.

You can guess how ridiculous it would have been for me to have my fortune told in a café. So I requested the pretty young witch to allow me to accompany her to her home; she agreed without demur, but she again wanted to know what time it was, and requested me to make my watch chime once more.

"Is it really in gold?" she asked, gazing at it a bit too attentively.

When we stepped out, night had completely fallen; most of the shops were closed, and the streets were almost deserted. We crossed the bridge over the Guadalquivir, and at the far end of that part of town we stopped outside a house that looked anything but palatial. A child opened the door to us. The *gitana* said to him a few words in a language I didn't recognize:

I later learnt it was Romani, or *chipe calli*, the language of the *gitanos*.* The child disappeared straight away, leaving us in a spacious room furnished with a small table, two stools and a trunk – and, before I forget, a water jug, a pile of oranges and a bunch of onions.

As soon as we were alone, the *gitana* went to her trunk and took out a pack of cards that seemed rather well worn, a magnet, a dried-up chameleon and a few other objects necessary to her art. Then she told me to cross my left palm with a coin, and the magical ceremonies began. It would be useless to relate her predictions, and as far as her modus operandi was concerned, it was obvious that she was a witch in the fullest sense of the term.

Unfortunately, we were soon interrupted. The door suddenly burst open, and a man, wrapped to the eyes in a brown cloak, came into the room pouring out a volley of ungracious abuse on the *gitana*. I couldn't understand what he was saying, but the tone of his voice indicated that he was in a really bad mood. The *gitana* seemed neither surprised nor angry to see him, but jumped up to meet him and, with extraordinary volubility, addressed him with a few phrases in the mysterious language she had already used in my presence. The word *payllo*, repeated several times, was the only word I could understand. I knew that it was the way *gitanos* designate any man from outside their own race. I assumed that I was the person she was referring to, and braced myself for a little chat about relationship matters. I had already got hold of the leg of one of the stools, and I was meditating on the question of when exactly would be the best time to throw it at the intruder's head. Meanwhile, he roughly pushed the *gitana* aside and came up to me – then, stepping back, he said:

"Ah, it's you, sir!"

I looked at him in turn, and recognized my friend Don José. Just then, I rather regretted not having allowed him to swing from the gallows.

"Ah, it's you, old fellow!" I exclaimed, giving a somewhat forced laugh. "You interrupted the young lady just as she was telling me some rather interesting things."

"Always the same! This has gone on long enough!" he said between his teeth, glaring at her.

Meanwhile, the *gitana* was continuing to speak to him in her language. She was gradually becoming more and more animated. Her eye was turning bloodshot and increasingly angry; her features were contorted, and she kept stamping her foot. She seemed to be urging him to do something he was hesitant to do. What she meant, I thought I understood only too well when I saw her motioning with her little hand quickly and repeatedly beneath her chin. I was inclined to believe that she was referring to a throat that needed to be cut, and I had a nasty suspicion that the throat in question might be mine.

To this great torrent of eloquence, Don José merely replied with two or three brusque words. Then the *gitana* darted a glance of deep contempt at him – and, sitting down cross-legged in a corner of the room, she selected an orange, peeled it and started to eat it.

Don José took me by the arm, opened the door and led me out into the street. We walked for about a hundred yards in the most profound silence. Then, waving his hand to show the direction, he said:

"Carry straight on, and you'll get to the bridge."

Whereupon he turned his back on me and rapidly walked away. I returned to my lodging feeling rather sheepish and somewhat irritated. The worst thing about it was that, as I was getting undressed, I discovered that my watch was missing.

Various considerations restrained me from going to ask for it the following day, or requesting that the local *corregidor** kindly order his men to search for it. I completed my work on the Dominicans' manuscript and left for Seville. After several months wandering across Andalusia, I decided to return to Madrid, and I had to pass through Córdoba. I didn't intend to stay there long, since I'd developed quite an aversion to that fine city and the bathing beauties of the Guadalquivir. However, a few friends I needed to see, and a few errands I had to carry out, were to keep me for at least three or four days in the ancient capital of the Muslim princes.

As soon as I showed up again at the Dominican monastery, one of the Fathers, who had always taken a great interest in my research on the exact site of Munda, greeted me with open arms, exclaiming:

"Praised be the name of the Lord! Welcome, welcome, my dear friend! We all thought you were dead, and as I stand here talking to you, I recited so many *Paters* and *Aves* – not that I regret them in the least – for the salvation of your soul. So you weren't murdered, then? Though we know that you *were* robbed."

"How do you know that?" I asked, a bit taken aback.

"Yes, *you* know – that fine repeating watch you used to set off chiming in the library when we told you it was time for the service to begin. Well, it's been found! You'll soon have it back."

"Er… well, actually," I interrupted, a little shamefacedly, "I'd mislaid it…"

"The scoundrel is under lock and key, and as he was well known as the type of man capable of taking a potshot at a decent Christian to relieve him of a peseta or two, we were mortally afraid that he'd killed you. I'll go with you to see the *corregidor*, and we'll get your fine watch back for you. And then just you dare to say, when you're back home, that the officers of justice don't do their job properly in Spain!"

"I have to confess," I told him, "that I'd rather lose my watch than give evidence which might get some poor devil hanged – especially as… as…"

"Oh, have no fear! He already comes with the highest recommendations for the gallows, and he can't be hanged twice. When I say 'hanged', I'm mistaken. He's a *hidalgo*, that thief of yours, so he's going to be garrotted,* the day after tomorrow, without remission. You see, in his case, one theft more or less won't change a thing. Would to God he'd done nothing worse than steal! But he's committed several murders, each one more horrible than the last."

"What's his name?"

"He's known in the locality as José Navarro, but he also has a Basque name, which neither you nor I will ever be able to pronounce. Look: he's a man worth seeing, and since you enjoy familiarizing yourself with the particularities of our country, you shouldn't lose a chance of learning how, in Spain, scoundrels take their leave of this life. He's in the chapel,* and Father Martínez will take you there."

My Dominican insisted so vehemently on my seeing the preparations for the "leuvely leetle execution"* that I was forced to accept. I went to visit the prisoner, having provided myself with a packet of cigars that, I hoped, would persuade him to excuse my indiscretion.

I was brought in to see Don José just as he was taking his meal. He gave me a somewhat curt nod, and thanked me politely for the gift I had brought. After counting the cigars in the packet I'd handed to him, he chose a certain number and returned the rest to me, observing that he wouldn't be needing more than that.

I asked him whether, with a little money, or through the influence of my friends, I could make his fate any easier. At first he shrugged, smiling sadly, but he soon changed his mind and asked me to have a mass said for the salvation of his soul.

"Would you also," he added shyly, "have another mass said for a person who offended you?"

"Of course, dear fellow," I said, "but as far as I know, there's nobody from round here who's ever offended me." He took my hand and squeezed it, looking grave. After a moment's silence, he continued:

"Can I presume to ask you for one more service? When you return home to your country, perhaps you'll pass through Navarre – at least, you'll go through Vittoria,* which isn't very far."

"Yes," said I, "I'll certainly be going through Vittoria, but it's quite possible I may go out of my way to see Pamplona, and I think I'd happily make the detour for your sake."

"Well then, if you do go to Pamplona, you'll see more than one thing of interest to you... It's a fine town... I'll give you this medallion" – he showed me a small silver medallion he was wearing round his neck. "You can wrap this in paper..." He stopped for a moment to get a grip on his feelings. "And... you can give it, or make sure it gets given, to a good woman whose address I'll give you. You can say I'm dead – you needn't say how."

I promised to perform his errand. I visited him the next day, and spent part of the day with him. It is from his lips that I learnt of the tragic adventure that you are about to read.

III

I was born – he told me – in Elizondo, in the Baztan valley.* My name is Don José Lizarrabengoa, and you know Spain well enough, sir, for my name to tell you straight away that I'm a Basque and an Old Christian.* If I assume the title Don, it's because I've a right to do so, and if I was in Elizondo I'd show you my family tree on parchment. They wanted me to go into the Church, and they made me study, but I didn't get much out of it. I enjoyed playing pelota* too much – that was my downfall. When we Navarrese play pelota, we forget about everything else. One day, when I'd won, a lad from Álava* picked a fight with me over the result; we took up our *maquilas*,* and I won yet again, but I was obliged to leave the area as a result. I met some dragoons, and signed up in the Almansa regiment,* cavalry division. Men from our mountains easily learn military ways. I soon became a corporal, and they'd promised to make me a sergeant when, as my ill luck would have it, I was sent to stand guard at the tobacco factory in Seville. If you've ever been to Seville, you'll have seen that big building outside the ramparts, near the Guadalquivir. In my mind, I can still see the main door and the guardroom next to it. When they're on duty, Spanish soldiers play cards or sleep – me, like a proper Navarrese, I always tried to find something to keep me busy. I was making a chain with brass wire to hold my priming pin. Suddenly, my mates start saying, "Listen, the bell's ringing – the girls'll be coming back to work."

As you must know, sir, there are a good four or five hundred women employed in the factory. They're the ones who roll the cigars in a big hall, where men aren't allowed in without permission from Mr Twenty-Four,* since they tend to strip off a bit, especially the young ones, when the weather's hot. When it's time for the girls to come back to work after their dinner, plenty of young men come to watch them go by, and hoot and whistle after them. Not many of those ladies will turn down a taffeta mantilla, and an experienced fisherman only needs to lean down and scoop up his catch. While the others were watching, I stayed put on my bench, near the door. I was young then – I was always thinking about home, and in my view the only pretty girls were those with blue skirts and plaits falling down to their shoulders.* In any case, I was scared of Andalusian women: I still hadn't got used to the way they behaved – always mocking, never a sensible word. So there I was, intent on my chain, when I heard some townsmen saying, "There's the *gitanilla*."* I looked up, and saw her. It was a Friday, and I'll never forget. I saw Carmen, the same woman that you know – it was her place where I met you a few months ago.

She was wearing a very short red skirt that showed her white silk stockings with more than one hole in them, and dainty little shoes of red morocco leather tied with flame-coloured ribbons. She'd pulled her mantilla open to show off her shoulders and the big bunch of acacia sticking out of her blouse. She had an acacia flower in the corner of her mouth, too, and walked along swaying her hips like a filly from the Córdoba stud farm.

In my region, everyone would have made the sign of the cross on seeing a woman dressed like that. In Seville, everyone paid her some suggestive compliment on her alluring appearance. She replied to each one in turn, giving them a sidelong glance, hand on hip, as brazen as the true *gitana* she was. At first I didn't like her, and I carried on with my work, but, following the custom of women and cats who don't come when you call them, but do come when you don't, she stopped in front of me and spoke to me.

"Hey, *compadre*,"* she said in the Andalusian way, "will you give me your chain to keep the keys to my trunk on?"

"It's to tie my priming pin to," I told her.

"Your priming pin!" she exclaimed with a hoot of laughter. "Ooh, sir must be making lace if he needs pins!"

Everyone burst out laughing, and I felt myself blush, and couldn't think of anything to say in reply.

"Come on, then, sweetheart," she continued, "make me seven ells of black lace for a mantilla, you darling little pinmaker!"

And, taking the acacia flower she had clamped in her mouth, she flicked it over at me with her thumb. It landed right between my eyes. It had the same effect on me, sir, as a bullet hitting me... I didn't know where to put myself: I just sat there stiff as a plank of wood. When she'd gone into the factory, I saw the acacia flower that had fallen to the ground between my feet. I don't know what came over me, but I picked it up without my friends noticing and placed it devoutly in my jacket. My first stupid mistake!

Two or three hours later, I'd forgotten all about it, when into the guardroom rushes a porter, puffing and panting, dismay written all over his face. He told us that in the big cigar hall a woman had been murdered, and the guards would have to go and sort it out. The sergeant told me to take two men and go and see what was up. So I take my men and make my way up there. Imagine, sir, that on entering the hall the first thing I find is three hundred women stripped to their underwear, or not much more, all yelling, howling, waving their arms about and making such a din you wouldn't have heard God's own thunder. On the one side, there was a woman lying with her arms and legs in the air, covered in blood, with an X on her face that someone had just cut into it with two knife slashes. Opposite the victim, who was being given assistance by the kinder women in the crowd, I see Carmen being held by five or six chattering hussies. The wounded woman kept shouting, "A priest! A priest! I'm dying!" Carmen said nothing: she clenched her teeth, and rolled her eyes like a chameleon.

"What's all this, then?" I asked. It was no easy business finding out what had happened, as all the factory girls started talking to me at once. It seems the wounded woman had been boasting about having enough money in her pocket to buy a donkey at the Triana market.*

"Get that!" Carmen had said – she could be pretty sharp-tongued. "Isn't a broomstick enough for you, then?"

The other woman, stung by the jibe, perhaps because it touched a sore point, replied that she didn't know much about broomsticks, not having the honour to be a Gypsy girl or Satan's god-daughter, but that Miss Carmencita would soon get to know her donkey, when the *corregidor* took her out riding, and two lackeys following along with whisks to shoo the flies off her.*

"Well, *I'm* going to carve some nice little holes in your cheek for those flies to drink from," said Carmen, "and just let me paint a draughts board on it."* No sooner said than "swish, swish!" – she picks up the knife she used for cutting the ends of the cigars with and started slicing St Andrew's crosses into the woman's face.

The case was clear. I took Carmen by the arm.

"Sister," I said politely, "you're going to have to come with me." She shot me a glance as if she recognized me, but she said resignedly, "Let's go. Where's my mantilla?"

She put it over her head in such a way that only one of her two big eyes showed, and followed both my men as docile as a sheep. When we reached the guardroom, the sergeant said it was a serious matter, and she'd have to be taken to the jail. It was me again who was obliged to take her. I placed her between two dragoons and marched behind as a corporal should in such circumstances. We set off in the direction of town. To begin with, the *gitana* had kept silent, but in the Calle Sierpes – you know the one, it deserves its name, given all its twists and turns* – in the Calle Sierpes, she starts by letting her mantilla fall to her shoulders, so as to show me her pretty little wheedling face, and, twisting round to me as much as she could, she said:

"So, where are you taking me to, officer?"

"Off to jail, my poor child," I replied as gently as I could, the way a good soldier should talk to a prisoner, especially a woman.

"Oh dear – whatever will become of me? Mr Officer, take pity on me. You're so young, so nice and kind!…" Then, in a lower tone, "Let me escape," she said, "and I'll give you a piece of *bar lachi* that'll make all the women fall in love with you."

Bar lachi, sir, is lodestone – the *gitanos* claim that you can perform all sorts of spells with it when you know how to use it. Give a woman a glass of white wine with a pinch of grated lodestone in it, she won't resist you any more. But I replied to her, as seriously as I could:

"We're not here to talk nonsense – you're off to prison. Orders is orders: end of story."

Those of us from the Basque country have an accent that makes it easy for the Spanish to recognize us – on the other hand, not one of them can even manage to say *baï, jaona*.* So Carmen had no difficulty guessing that I came from the provinces.* As you'll know, sir, the *gitanos*, having no homeland, and being always on the move, speak every language, and most of them are at home in Portugal, in France, in the provinces, in Catalonia, everywhere

– even with the Moors and the English they manage to make themselves understood. Carmen knew Basque pretty well.

"*Laguna*,* *ene bihotsarena*," she suddenly said: "Friend of my heart, are you from our part of the world?"

Our language, sir, is so beautiful that when we hear it in a foreign land, it makes us shiver with delight...

("I'd like to have a confessor from the provinces," the bandit added in a lower tone. Then, after a silence, he resumed his story.)

"I'm from Elizondo," I told her in Basque, deeply moved to hear her speak my language.

"And I'm from Echalar,"* she said. (This is a village about four hours from my own.) "I was brought to Seville by the *gitanos*. I was working in the factory to earn enough to return to Navarre and live with my old mother, who only has me to provide for her, and a little *barratcea** with twenty apple trees for cider. Ah, if only I was back home, at the foot of the white mountain!* They insulted me just because I don't come from this land of crooks and pedlars of rotten oranges – and those bitches all ganged up against me because I told them that all their Seville *jacques*,* knives and all, wouldn't frighten a lad from home with his blue beret and his *maquila*. Be a pal, my friend – won't you do something for a girl from back home?"

She was lying, sir – she always lied. I don't know if that girl ever said a single true word in her life, but when she spoke, I believed her: I couldn't help myself. Her Basque was lousy, and yet I thought she was from Navarre – just from her eyes and her mouth and her lips you could tell she was a *gitana*. I was crazy – I'd stopped thinking straight. I reckoned that if any Spaniards had taken it into their heads to slag off *my* homeland, I'd have sliced their faces open the same way as she'd just done to her colleague. Anyway, I was like a drunk – I was starting to say silly things, and I was on the verge of doing something just as silly.

"If I was to push you and you fell over, my friend," she said in Basque, "these two soldier boys from Castille wouldn't be able to stop me..."

God help me, I forgot about orders and everything else, and told her, "Fair enough, sweetheart – since you're from back home, go for it, and may Our Lady of the Mountain help you!"

Just then we were marching past one of those narrow backstreets you find everywhere in Seville. Suddenly, Carmen turns round and gives me a punch in the stomach. I deliberately pretended to fall over backwards. In a single bound she jumps right over me and starts to leg it... They say "legs of a Basque": hers were as good as anyone else's – nice and fast, and shapely with it. I immediately get up again, but I make sure my lance* gets in the way and blocks the street so that, to begin with, it stopped my mates chasing after her. Then I myself started to run, and they came running after me, but as for catching up with her... There was no chance of that happening, with our spurs, our sabres and our lances! In less time than it takes to tell it, our captive had vanished. In any case, all the old girls in the district did their bit to help her escape, and pulled the wool over our eyes, telling us to go the wrong way. After a lot of travelling back and forth, we finally had to return to the guardhouse without any receipt to say we'd delivered her to the prison governor.

To avoid being punished, my men said that Carmen had spoken to me in Basque – and it didn't seem entirely natural, to tell the truth, that a punch from such a petite young thing could have so easily floored a strong and sturdy lad like me. It all seemed a bit suspicious – or, rather, perfectly clear. When I came off duty, I was demoted and sent to jail for a month. This was my first punishment ever since I'd been in the army. I could kiss goodbye to the sergeant's stripes I'd thought were already in my grasp!

My first days in prison were really pretty grim. When I'd become a soldier, I'd thought that I'd get to be made an officer at the very least. After all, Longa and Mina, my compatriots, are captain generals; Chapalangarra – who's a "black" like Mina, and like him a refugee in your country – Chapalangarra was a colonel, and I'd played pelota a score of times with his brother, a poor devil like me.* Now I started to say to myself, "All the time you served without getting into trouble has been wasted. Now you've blotted your copybook – to get back into the good graces of the bosses, you'll have to work ten times harder than when you signed on! And what have I gone and got myself punished for? For a pert little *gitana* who made a fool of me and who, this very minute, is busy playing the thief in some part of town or other."

All the same, I couldn't stop thinking about her. Would you believe it, sir? Her silk stockings, full of holes, that she gave me an eyeful of as she legged it – well, I could still see them right in front of my eyes. I gazed through the prison bars out at the street, and, of all the women going by, I didn't see a single one who was worth that minx. And then, in spite of myself, I could smell that acacia flower she'd thrown to me: it had dried up, but it had kept all its perfume... If there *are* such things as witches, that girl was one of them!

One day, in comes the jailer, and gives me a small loaf of Alcalá* bread.

"Here," he said, "look what your lady cousin's sent you."

I took the loaf, pretty surprised, since I didn't have a cousin in Seville. "Perhaps it's a mistake," I thought, gazing at the bread, but it gave me such an appetite and smelt so good that, without bothering where it had come from and who it was meant for, I decided to eat it. When I started cutting it, my knife encountered something hard. I took a closer look, and I found a small English file that had been slipped into the dough before the bread was baked. Also in the bread was hidden a two-piastre* gold coin. That removed any doubt: it was a present from Carmen. For people of her race, freedom is everything, and they'd set fire to a whole town rather than have to spend a single day in prison. And on top of that, she was a cunning lass, and this loaf gave her a chance to hoodwink the jailers.

Within an hour, the little file could have sawn its way through the thickest bar – and with the two-piastre coin, the minute I came across a second-hand-clothes dealer's, I'd have swapped my soldier's greatcoat for civvies. As you can guess, a man who'd more than once stolen eaglets from their nests up in the rocks wouldn't think twice about dropping down into the street from a window less than thirty feet above the ground – but I didn't want to escape. I still had my honour as a soldier, and deserting seemed a great crime to my mind. Still, I was touched by this sign that someone had remembered me. When you're in jail, you like to think you've got a friend outside who takes an interest in you. The gold coin offended me a bit – I'd really have liked to pay it back, but where could I find my creditor? That didn't seem very easy.

After the ceremony of being demoted, I didn't think I had anything more to go through – but there was still one humiliation I had to swallow. It was when I came out of jail and was put on duty again: I had to stand guard like an ordinary soldier. You can't imagine what a man with any guts or decency feels on occasions like that. I think I'd almost have preferred being shot. At least you march alone, at the head of your firing squad: you feel you're a somebody – everyone's eyes are on you.

I was made to stand guard at the colonel's door. He was a wealthy young chap, easygoing too – he liked to enjoy himself. All the young officers were round his place, and plenty of civilians... women too – actresses, so I gathered. In my view, it was as if the whole town had agreed to meet in front of his door just so as to take a look at me. Then up comes the colonel's carriage, with his valet on the seat. And what do I see getting out, if not *la gitanilla*? This time, she was as elaborately adorned as a saint's reliquary, all dolled up and rigged out with gold and ribbons everywhere. A sequined dress, blue shoes with sequins too, flowers and gold braid all over. She was holding a tambourine.* There were two other *gitanas* with her, an old one and a young one. There's always an old one to lead them – then an old man with a guitar, another *gitano*, to accompany them as they dance. As you know, people often like getting *gitanas* to perform in public, and make them dance the *romalis* – that's their dance – and other things too, more often than not.

Carmen recognized me, and we exchanged glances. I don't know why but, just then, I'd have given anything for the ground to swallow me up.

"*Agur laguna*,"* she said. "Officer, you're standing guard like a common soldier!" And before I could think of a word to say, she was already inside the house.

The whole company was in the courtyard, and, despite the crowd, I could see pretty much everything that was going on through the bars of the gate.* I could hear the castanets, the laughter and the cries of "Bravo!" – sometimes I caught sight of her head when she jumped into the air with her tambourine. Then I could hear some of the other officers saying various things to her that made me go red in the face. As for what she replied, I have no idea. It was that day, I think, that I started to love her really and truly – for, three or four times, I was on the point of giving in to temptation, going into the courtyard and sticking my sabre into the belly of all those conceited little squirts who were busy sweet-talking her. My torment lasted a good hour, then the *gitanos* left, and the carriage took them back. As she went by, Carmen looked at me once more with those eyes of hers that you're familiar with, and said in a very low voice, "Friend, those who like a nice plate of whitebait go to Lillas Pastia's in Triana." As light-footed as a kid goat, she bounded into the carriage, the driver whipped up his mules, and the whole merry band went off I don't know where.

As you'll have guessed, when I came off duty I headed to Triana – but first I went for a shave and gave myself a brush-down as if it were parade day. She was at Lillas Pastia's – he was an old whitebait seller, a *gitano*, as dusky as a blackamoor: it was at his place that many of the townspeople came to eat their whitebait – especially, I think, since Carmen had set up her quarters there.

"Lillas," she said, as soon as she saw me, "I'm taking the rest of the day off. Tomorrow's another day, eh?* Come on, my friend from back home, let's go for a walk."

She wrapped herself up to the nose in her mantilla, and there we were, out in the street, me not knowing where I was going.

"Miss," I said to her, "I guess I owe you a thank you for a certain present you sent me when I was in jail. I ate the bread; the file will be useful for sharpening my lance, and I'll keep it as a souvenir of you – but as for the money, here it is."

"Well, well... he kept the money!" she exclaimed, and burst out laughing. "A good thing too, now I think of it... I'm running a bit short. But so what? A dog on the prowl will soon find a fowl.* Come on, let's blow it all on a nice meal. You can treat me."

We'd started out on the road back to Seville. At the entry to the Calle Sierpes, she bought a dozen oranges, which she made me wrap up in my handkerchief. A little further on, she bought another loaf, some sausage and a bottle of manzanilla – finally, she went into a confectioner's. Here, she flung onto the counter the gold coin I'd given her back and another coin that she had in her pocket, plus some silver – in the end she asked me to give her everything I had. This was just one small coin and a few quarters, and I gave it all to her, quite ashamed not to have more. I thought she wanted to buy up the whole store. She took all the finest and most expensive things in it – *yemas*,* *turrón*,* crystallized fruit – everything she could afford, until the money ran out. And it was me again that had to carry it all in paper bags. You may know the Street of the Candilejo, where there's a stone head of King Don Pedro the Just.* This head should have made me think. We stopped in this street outside an old house. She went into the passage and knocked at the front door. A *gitana*, a real servant of Satan, came and opened up for us. Carmen spoke a few words of Romani to her. The old woman groused about it to begin with. To keep her happy, Carmen gave her a couple of oranges and a handful of sweets, and allowed her to have a slug of the wine. Then she placed her cloak over her back and led her to the door, which she closed with the wooden bar. As soon as we were alone, she started to dance and laugh like a madwoman, singing, "You are my *rom*, I am your *romi*."*

There I was in the middle of the room, still weighed down with all her purchases, and not knowing where to put them down. She dumped everything on the floor, and flung her arms round my neck, telling me, "I pay my debts – I pay my debts! That's the law of the *Calé*!"*

("Ah, sir," said Don José to me, "that day, that day!... When I remember it, I forget all about tomorrow."

The bandit fell silent for a moment – then, after relighting his cigar, he continued.)

We spent the whole day together – eating, drinking and all the rest of it. When she'd eaten as many sweets as a child of six, she stuffed handfuls of them into the old woman's water jug.

"It's to make sherbet for her," she said.

She crushed the *yemas* by throwing them against the wall.

"That's so the flies will leave us alone..." she said.

There wasn't a single silly game or trick she didn't get up to. I told her I'd like to see her dance, but where were we to get any castanets from? She straight away picked up the old woman's only plate, smashed it into pieces, and – lo and behold – she started dancing the *romalis*, clacking the earthenware fragments every bit as if she'd been playing castanets of ebony or ivory. There was never a dull moment with that girl, I promise you. Evening came, and I heard the drums beating the retreat.

"I've got to get back to barracks for roll call," I told her.

"Barracks?" she said scornfully. "So are you some kind of Negro slave, to let yourself be ruled by a rod of iron? You're a real canary, both in clothes and character.* Go on, then, if you want to be chicken-livered."

I stayed, resigned in advance to some time in the lockup. The next day, she was the first one to talk of us separating.

"Listen, Joseíto," she said, "have I paid you back? By our law, I owed you nothing, since you're a *payllo*, but you're a handsome lad, and I took a shine to you. Now we're quits. See you."

I asked her when I'd see her again.

"As soon as you're less of a ninny," she replied with a laugh. Then, more seriously, "D'you know, my son, I think I'm just a little bit in love with you? But it can't last. The lion may lie down with the lamb, but not for long. Perhaps, if you were to follow the law of Egypt,* I'd be happy to become your *romi*. But I'm just being silly: no way that'll happen. Pah! Believe you me, my lad, you're lucky to have got off so lightly. You've met the Devil – yes, the Devil! He's not always black, and he didn't break your neck. I may be dressed in wool, but I'm no sheep.* Go and light a candle to your *majari** – she's certainly earned it. Go on – goodbye again. Don't think about Carmencita, or she might get you to marry a certain old widow with a wooden leg."*

While she was saying this, she lifted the bar that held the door closed, and once in the street she wrapped herself up in her mantilla and turned on her heel.

She was right. It would have been wise for me not to think of her, but from that day in the Street of the Candilejo onwards I couldn't think of anything else. I prowled round day after day, hoping to bump into her. I asked the old woman and the whitebait seller for news of her. Both of them told me she'd left for Laloro,* which is what they called Portugal. Probably it was on Carmen's instructions that they told me this, but it wasn't long before I discovered they were lying. A few days after my day in the Street of the Candilejo, I was standing guard at one of the city gates. A short distance from this gate there was a breach that had been made in the city walls; they spent the daytime repairing it, and at night they set a sentry there to keep smugglers out. During the day, I saw Lillas Pastia coming and going repeatedly around the guardroom, and chatting with several of my mates – they all knew him, and they knew his fish and his fritters even better. He came up to me and asked me if I had any news of Carmen.

"No," I said.

"Well, you soon will, *compadre*."

He wasn't wrong. That night, I was put on sentry duty at the breach. As soon as the corporal had gone off, I saw a woman coming towards me. My heart told me it was Carmen. But I shouted:

"Keep back! No way through!"

"No need to be so nasty," she said, revealing her identity.

"What! You here, Carmen!"

"Yes, old chum.* Let's keep it short and sweet. Do you fancy earning yourself a duro?* Some people are going to turn up with a few packages – just let them get on with it."

"No," I said. "My duty is to try and stop them getting through. Orders is orders."

"Orders! Orders! You didn't think much about orders in the Street of the Candilejo."

"Ah," I said, overwhelmed by the mere memory of it. "It was worth my while to forget about orders then – but I don't want any money from smugglers."

"So, if you don't want money, would you like to come and have dinner again at old Dorotea's?"

"No!" I said, half choking with the effort it cost me. "I can't."

"Fine. If you're so difficult, I know who to turn to. I'll suggest to your officer that *he* comes to Dorotea's. He seems like an easygoing fellow, and he'll make sure the man on sentry duty is a reliable young chap who'll know how to turn a blind eye.

Goodbye, canary. I'll laugh loud and long the day that orders is orders... to hang you."

I had the weakness to call her back, and I promised to let the whole race of *gitanos* pass, if necessary, so long as I could obtain the only reward I wanted. She immediately swore she'd keep her word the very next day, and ran over to alert her friends, who were just a stone's throw away. There were five of them, including Pastia, all heavily laden with English merchandise. Carmen kept the lookout. She was supposed to warn them with her castanets as soon as she saw the patrol coming, but she didn't need to. The smugglers had done the necessary in the twinkling of an eye.

The next day, I went to the Street of the Candilejo. Carmen kept me waiting, and when she turned up, she was in a pretty bad mood.

"I don't like people who have to be asked twice," she said. "You did me a bigger favour the first time, when you didn't know you'd get anything out of it. Yesterday, you haggled with me. I don't know why I've come, since I don't love you any more. Look, clear off – here's a duro for your pains."

I nearly threw the coin in her face, and I was obliged to make a violent effort to stop myself giving her a thrashing. After we'd been quarrelling for about an hour, I left, feeling furious. I wandered for some time through the town, roaming this way and that like a madman – finally, I went into a church, and, having found the darkest corner to sit down in, I wept hot tears. Suddenly I heard a voice.

"Dragoon's tears, dragon's tears! I'll make a potion out of them."

I looked up, and there was Carmen in front of me.

"Well, old chum, you still mad at me?" she said. "I must be in love with you, in spite of myself, since ever since you left me I don't know what's been wrong with me. Come on, now it's me that's asking *you* if you want to come round to the Street of the Candilejo."

So we made up – but Carmen's mood was as fickle as the weather back home. In our mountains, the storm's never so close as when the sun is shining brightest. She'd promised to see me another day at Dorotea's, and she didn't turn up. And Dorotea told me even more brazenly that she'd gone to Laloro on Egyptian business.

As experience had already taught me to take such a statement with a pinch of salt, I looked for Carmen wherever I thought she might be, and I passed twenty times a day down the Street of the Candilejo. One evening, I was at Dorotea's – I'd almost got her at my beck and call, buying her a glass of anisette from time to time – when Carmen came in, followed by a young man, a lieutenant in our regiment.

"Get lost, this minute," she told me in Basque.

I was dumbfounded, and my heart was seething.

"What the hell do you think you're doing here?" said the lieutenant. "Go on, hop it!"

I couldn't take a single step: it was as if I was paralysed. The officer, enraged to see that I wasn't leaving, and that I hadn't even taken off my soldier's cap, seized me by the collar and shook me roughly. I don't know what I said to him. He drew his sword, and I unsheathed mine. The old woman grabbed me by the arm, and the lieutenant slashed me on the forehead: I still bear the scar. I recoiled, and shoved Dorotea over with my elbow – then, as the lieutenant was charging after me, I held out my sword point to his body, and he impaled himself. Then Carmen blew out the lamp, and in her language told Dorotea to run for it. As for me, I escaped into the street, and started to run without knowing where I was going. It seemed as if someone was following me. When I came to my senses, I found that Carmen hadn't left me.

"You stupid ninny of a canary!" she said. "You only ever do the most idiotic things. And I *told* you I'd bring you bad luck. Come on, when there's a will there's a way – at least when you've got a Flemish Romani lass* as your sweetheart. Start by tying this handkerchief round your head, and throw that belt over to me. Wait for me in this alley. I'll be back in two minutes."

She vanished, and soon brought me back a striped cloak that she'd picked up Heaven knows where. She made me strip off my uniform and put on the cloak over my shirt. Thus attired, with the handkerchief she had used to bandage my head wound, I rather resembled a Valencian peasant, of the kind you see in Seville, who come to sell their *chufas** barley water. Then she led me into a house quite similar to Dorotea's, at the far end of an alleyway. She and another *gitana* washed me, bandaged me better than an army surgeon would have done and gave me I don't know what to drink – finally, they made me lie on a mattress, and I went to sleep.

Those women had probably mixed into my drink a few of those drugs that only they know about, the ones that make you sleepy, since it was late the next day before I woke up. I had a bad headache and a bit of a temperature. It was some time before it all came back to me – that terrible scene I'd been involved in the night before. After binding my wound, Carmen and her friend, both squatting on their heels next to my mattress, exchanged a few words in *chipe calli* – it was like they were holding a medical consultation. Then they both assured me that I'd be over it before long, but I needed to leave Seville as soon as possible, since if I was found there, I'd be shot, and no chance of mercy.

"My lad," said Carmen, "you've got to do something. Now that the king isn't going to provide you with rice or hake,* you ought to think about earning your living. You're too dumb to steal *à pastesas** – but you're nimble and strong: if you've got the stomach for it, head for the coast, and make a smuggler of yourself. Didn't I promise I'd get you hanged? It's better than getting shot. And anyway, if you know how to go about it, you can live like a prince for as long as the *miñones** and the coastguards don't manage to collar you."

It was in this engaging fashion that this devil of a girl showed me the new career she had in mind for me – the only one, truth to tell, that was still open to me now that I'd incurred the death penalty. I don't mind confessing to you, sir, that she didn't have much trouble persuading me. I felt I was getting much more intimately close to her through this life of risk and rebellion. From then on, I felt assured of her love. I'd often heard people talking about the smugglers who roamed through Andalusia astride their fine horses, gripping their blunderbusses, with their mistresses riding behind the saddle. I could see myself already trotting up hill and down dale with the nice *gitana* lady behind me. When I said as much to her, she uttered a side-splitting laugh and told me there was nothing so fine as a night spent out bivouacking, when every *rom* goes off with his *romi* into his little tent made out of three hoops with a blanket thrown over them.

"If I ever get you up into the mountains," I told her, "I'll be sure of you! Up there, there's no lieutenant to share you with."

"Ah! You're jealous," she said. "Too bad for you. How can you be so silly? Can't you see I love you, since I've never asked you for any money?"

When she spoke like that, she made me want to strangle her.

To cut a long story short, sir, Carmen picked up some civilian clothes for me, so I could leave Seville without being recognized. I went to Jerez with a letter from Pastia for an anisette merchant whose house was used as the smugglers' rendezvous. I was introduced to them – their leader, nicknamed El Dancaire,* took me into his gang. We set out for Gaucín,* where I met up with Carmen, who'd arranged to see me there. On expeditions, she acted as a spy for our gang, and there was never a better spy than her. She was on her way back from Gibraltar, and she'd already arranged with a ship's captain to put on board some English merchandise that we were to pick up on the coast. We went to wait for it near Estepona, then we hid part of it in the mountains. Loaded with the rest, we went on to Ronda. Carmen had gone there ahead of us. She was again the one who told us the best time to enter the town. This first expedition and several later ones were all successful. The smuggler's life pleased me more than the soldier's; I could give Carmen presents. I had money and a mistress. I didn't feel much remorse, since, as the *gitanos* say, the scabs that give you pleasure do not itch.* Everywhere we were given a good reception; my companions treated me well, and even showed me a certain respect. The reason was that I'd killed a man, and among them were some who didn't have a similar exploit on their consciences. But the biggest advantage of my new life was the fact I got to see Carmen so often. She was friendlier towards me than ever – and yet, in front of our comrades, she wouldn't go along with the idea that she was my mistress, and she'd even made me swear every kind of oath that I wouldn't tell them a thing about her. I was so weak-willed with that hussy that I obeyed her every whim. In any case, this was the first time she'd shown me she could have the reserve of a decent, honest woman, and I was simple enough to believe that she'd really become a better person, no longer so prone to her earlier moods.

Our gang, composed of eight or ten men, hardly ever met except at the decisive moments, and we were usually scattered by twos or threes through the towns and villages. Each of us made out he had a trade: one was an ironmonger, another a horse dealer. I was a haberdasher, but I hardly showed my face in the bigger towns after that nasty business of mine in Seville. One day, or rather one night, we'd agreed to meet south of Vejer.* El Dancaire and I found that we'd got there before the rest. He seemed extremely cheerful.

"We're going to have an extra mate," he told me. "Carmen has just pulled off one of her best and bravest jobs. She's just got her *rom* out: he was in the *presidio* at Tarifa."*

I was already starting to understand the Romani language, as almost all my mates spoke it, and this word "*rom*" gave me quite a start.

"What! Her husband! You mean she's married?" I asked the captain.

"Yes," he said, "to One-Eyed García, a *gitano* lad as sly as she is. The poor chap was in the galleys. Carmen cleverly hoodwinked the *presidio* surgeon and managed to spring her *rom*. Ah, that girl's worth her weight in gold! It was two years ago she started trying to get him out. Nothing worked, until they decided the best thing was to change the medical officer – and with *him*, it seems she soon found a way of reaching an understanding."

You can imagine my delight at this news. I soon saw One-Eyed García – he was quite the ugliest monster that the *gitano* world has ever bred: his skin was black, and his soul blacker, and he was the most out-and-out villain I've ever encountered in my life. Carmen came with him – and when she called him her *rom* in front of me, you should have seen the eyes she started making at me, and the face she pulled when García looked round. It made me angry, and I didn't speak to her all night. The next morning we'd made up our bundles, and we were already on our way when we realized that a dozen horsemen were hot on our heels. The cocky Andalusians, who were always talking about massacring everyone, immediately started looking a bit crestfallen. There was a general stampede. Only El Dancaire, García, a handsome lad from Écija who was called El Remendado* and Carmen didn't lose their heads. The rest had abandoned the mules and jumped down into the ravines, where the horses wouldn't be able to follow them. We couldn't keep our mounts, and we hurriedly unloaded the best part of our booty, and slung it over our shoulders – then we tried to escape over the rocks, down the steepest slopes. We threw our bundles ahead of us, and followed them the best we could, slipping and sliding down on our heels. Meanwhile, the enemy was sniping at us. This was the first time I'd ever heard balls whizzing by, and I wasn't particularly frightened. When a woman's keeping her eyes on you, there's no great merit in mocking death. We all escaped, except poor Remendado, who got a bullet in the small of his back. I dropped my load and went to try and carry him.

"You idiot!" shouted García. "What's the point of going to help a dead dog? Finish him off, and don't lose the cotton stockings."

"Drop him! Drop him!" Carmen kept shouting.

Exhaustion forced me to put him down for a minute in the shelter of a rock. García came up, and fired his blunderbuss point blank at his head.

"It would be a clever chap as could recognize him now," he said, gazing at the face that twelve balls had blown to shreds.

You can see, sir, what a fine life I led. In the evening, we found ourselves in a thicket, completely worn out, with nothing to eat, and ruined by the loss of our mules. What did that devil García do? He took a pack of cards out of his pocket and started to play a game with El Dancaire by the light of a fire that they'd lit. Meanwhile, I myself had lain down, gazing at the stars, thinking about Remendado and telling myself I'd just as well be in his place. Carmen was crouched down near me, and from time to time she'd rattle her castanets and hum. Then, coming over as if to say something into my ear, she kissed me, despite my reluctance, two or three times.

"You're the Devil," I told her.

"Yes," she replied.

After a few hours' rest, she went off to Gaucín, and the next morning a little goatherd came to bring us some bread. We stayed there all day long, and at night we made our way to the vicinity of Gaucín. We waited for news of Carmen. Nothing came. When day came, we saw a muleteer leading a well-dressed woman with a parasol and a little girl who seemed to be her domestic servant. García said to us:

"Look, two mules and two women that St Nicholas is sending us. I'd prefer four mules... Too bad, this'll do!"

He took his blunderbuss and headed down towards the path, hiding in the scrub. We followed him, El Dancaire and me, a short distance away. When we came within reach, we jumped up and shouted to the muleteer to stop. The woman, on seeing us, instead of taking fright – and our outfit would have been quite enough to scare her – burst out laughing.

"Ah! The *lillipendi* think I'm an *erani*!"* It was Carmen, but so well disguised that I'd never have recognized her if she'd been speaking any other language. She jumped down off her mule and spoke for a while with El Dancaire and García, and then said to me, "Canary, we'll meet again before you get hanged. I'm going to Gibraltar on Egyptian business. You'll all soon be hearing from me."

We separated, after she'd given us details of a place where we could find shelter for a few days. This girl was the lifeblood of our gang. We soon received some money which she'd sent to us, and a piece of advice that was even more valuable: on such and such a day, two English lords would be leaving Gibraltar for Granada by such and such a road. We took the hint. They had some fine and splendid guineas with them. García wanted to kill them, but El Dancaire and I were opposed to the idea. We only took their money and their watches, apart from the shirts, which we were greatly in need of.

Sir, a man can turn into a rogue without even thinking about it. A pretty girl makes you lose your head: you get into a fight over her; there's a nasty accident; you have to live in the mountains – you start out as a smuggler, and before you've even thought about it you've turned into a thief. We decided it wouldn't be very healthy for us to hang around near Gibraltar after this business with the English lords, and we headed deep into the Sierra de Ronda.

You mentioned José María to me – well, it was there that I got to know him. He took his mistress on his expeditions. She was a pretty girl – sensible, modest, with good manners... never an uncivil word, and such devotion!... But he repaid her by making her really unhappy. He was always chasing all the other girls – he'd treat her roughly, and then he'd take it into his head to get jealous. One time, he lashed out at her with a dagger. Well, she merely loved him all the more. That's how women are, especially Andalusian women. This one was proud of the scar she had on her arm, and showed it off as if it were the finest thing in the world. And then José María, into the bargain, was the worst mate you could imagine... In one expedition that we did, he so arranged matters that all the profit went to him, while we picked up all the cuts and bruises and nothing but vexations for our pains. But I'll get on with my story. We heard no more about Carmen. El Dancaire said, "One of us will have to go to Gibraltar for news of her – she must be up to some business or other. I'd happily go, but I'm too well known in Gibraltar."

One-Eye said, "Me too, they know me there – I've played too many dirty tricks on the Lobsters!* And as I've only got one eye, it's difficult to disguise me."

"So it'll have to be me that goes?" I said in turn, delighted at the mere idea of seeing Carmen again. "Fair enough – what do I need to do?"

The others told me:

"So you just need to jump into a boat, or go over by way of San Roque, as you prefer, and when you get to Gibraltar, ask in the port where a chocolate seller by the name of Rollona* lives. When you find her, you can ask her what's happening over there."

It was agreed that we'd all three set out for the Sierra de Gaucín: I'd leave my two mates there and travel to Gibraltar in the guise of a fruit merchant. In Ronda, a man who was in cahoots with us had managed to get me a passport; in Gaucín, I was given a donkey; I loaded it with oranges and melons, and set out. Once I'd reached Gibraltar, I discovered that everyone knew Rollona, but she was dead or else had gone off to *finibus terræ*,* and her disappearance explained, in my view, how we'd come to lose our means of correspondence with Carmen. I left my donkey in a stable, and, taking my oranges, I went round the town as if to sell them, but really in order to see whether I might perhaps bump into someone whose face I'd recognize. All the scum from every country in the world gather there, and it's a real Tower of Babel, since you can't walk ten steps in a street without hearing as many languages. I could see plenty of Egyptian folk, but I hardly dared trust them; I sounded them out, and they did the same to me. We easily guessed we were all scoundrels – the important thing was to find out if we were in the same gang. After two days of useless roaming around, I'd learnt nothing about Rollona or Carmen, and I was starting to think I'd make a few purchases and get back to my mates, when, as I was walking down a street at sunset, I hear a woman's voice from a window saying to me, "Mr Orange-Seller!..."

I looked up, and there on a balcony I saw Carmen leaning on the balcony with an officer in red, with golden epaulettes, curly hair and the bearing of some grand English lord. As for her, she was dressed superbly: a shawl over her shoulders, a golden comb and silk from head to toe – and the same fine figure of a woman she always was, laughing fit to burst. The Englishman, in his broken Spanish, shouted to me to come up, as madam wanted some oranges, and Carmen said to me in Basque, "Come up, and don't show any surprise."

Nothing, indeed, could surprise me, coming from her. I don't know whether seeing her again gave me more pleasure or pain. There was at the door a grand English servant, all powdered, who led me into a magnificent salon. Carmen immediately said to me in Basque: "You don't know a word of Spanish – you don't know me." Then, turning to the Englishman:

"I told you so, I immediately recognized he was a Basque. Now you'll hear just what a funny language it is. He looks quite stupid, don't you think? Makes you think of a cat caught at it in the larder."

"And you," I told her in my own language, "you look like a brazen hussy, and I have half a mind to slash your face in front of your lover boy."

"Lover boy!" she said. "So did you work that out all by yourself? And you're jealous of *this* idiot? You're even more of a ninny than you were before our nights in the Street of the Candilejo. Can't you see, you bonehead, that right now I'm engaged on Egyptian business? And it's going absolutely brilliantly. This house is mine; the Lobster's guineas will soon be mine. I'm leading him by the nose – I'm going to lead him somewhere he won't ever get out of."

"Look," I said, "if you do Egyptian business this way again, *I'll* make sure it's the last business you ever do."

"Oh, sure! Are you my *rom*, to order me around? One-Eye thinks it's all right, so what business is it of yours? Shouldn't you be content to be the only one who can call himself my *minchorrò*?"*

"What's he saying?" asked the Englishman.

"He's saying he's thirsty and he'd like a drink," replied Carmen.

And she flung herself down on a sofa, breaking out into a peal of laughter at her own translation.

Sir, when that girl started laughing, there was no way you could talk sensibly. Everyone else started laughing with her. That grand Englishman also started to laugh, like the idiot he was, and ordered that I be brought a drink.

While I was drinking, she said, "Do you see that ring he's wearing? If you like, I'll give it to you."

I replied, "I'd give a finger to get your English lord up in the mountains, each of us with a *maquila* in our hands."

"*Maquila* – what does that mean?" asked the Englishman.

"*Maquila*," said Carmen, still laughing, "is an orange.* Isn't it a funny word for an orange? He says he'd like to see you eating an orange."

"Yes?" said the Englishman. "Very well! Bring some more oranges tomorrow."

As we were talking, the servant came in and said that dinner was ready. Then the Englishman got up, gave me a piastre and offered his arm to Carmen, as if she wasn't capable of walking by herself. Carmen, still laughing, said to me, "My lad, I can't invite you to dinner, but tomorrow, as soon as you hear the drum beating for the parade, come here with your oranges. You'll find a bedroom better furnished than the one in the Street of the Candilejo, and you'll see if I'm still your Carmencita. And then we'll talk Egyptian business."

I didn't reply, and I was out in the street when the Englishman shouted after me, "Bring some *maquila* tomorrow!" – and I again heard Carmen's peals of laughter.

I left not knowing what I'd do – I hardly slept, and in the morning I felt so angry at that two-timing woman that I made up my mind to leave Gibraltar without seeing her again. But at the first roll of the drum, all my courage abandoned me: I picked up my string of oranges and I rushed over to Carmen's. Her shutter was half open, and I could see her big dark eyes looking out for me. The powdered servant let me in immediately. Carmen gave him an errand, and as soon as we were alone, she burst out into one of her crocodile laughs* and flung her arms round me. I'd never seen her looking so beautiful. Adorned like a madonna, perfumed... silken furnishings, embroidered curtains... ah... and me looking like the thief I was.

"*Minchorrò!*" said Carmen. "I've got half a mind to trash this place, set fire to the whole house and escape up into the sierra."

And then there were such terms of affection!... And such laughter!... And she danced, and she tore her frills and flounces: never did a monkey gambol more, pull more faces or get up to more mischief – little devil! Then she became serious once again, and said, "Listen: top of the agenda is Egyptian matters. I want him to take me to Ronda, where I've got a sister who's a nun..." Another peal of laughter. "We're passing through a place I'll tell you. You'll attack him – strip him bare! The best would be to bump him off,

48

but," she added with the diabolical smile that she had at certain moments (and *that* smile was something nobody felt inclined to imitate), "do you know what you ought to do? Let One-Eye come up first. You keep back a bit: the Lobster is brave and skilful – he has good pistols... Catch my drift?..." She broke off, with a new burst of laughter that made me shudder.

"No," I said. "I hate García, but he's my mate. One day, perhaps, I'll get rid of him for you, but we'll settle our accounts the way we do in my country. It's pure chance if I'm an Egyptian now – and when it comes to certain things, I'll always be a true Navarrese,* as the phrase goes."

She went on: "You're a fool, a ninny, a real *payllo*. You're like the dwarf who thinks he's tall just because he can spit a long way.* You don't love me: go on, get lost."

When she told me to get lost, I couldn't. I promised to leave, to go back to my mates and wait for the Englishman. For her part, she promised to go sick until it was time to leave Gibraltar for Ronda. I stayed another two days in Gibraltar. She had the nerve to come and see me in the inn where I was staying. She was in disguise. I left – I'd got plans of my own. I returned to our pre-arranged meeting place: I knew the time and the place that the Englishman and Carmen were due to pass. I found El Dancaire and García waiting for me. We spent the night in a wood, round a pine-cone fire that provided a merry blaze. I offered García a game of cards. He accepted. At the second game, I told him he was cheating. He started to laugh. I flung the cards in his face. He reached for his blunderbuss. I stepped on it and told him:

"They say you can handle a knife as well as the best cut-throat in Málaga. Fancy taking me on?"

El Dancaire tried to separate us. I'd already landed two or three punches on García. Anger had spurred him on – he'd drawn his knife, and I'd drawn mine. We told El Dancaire to get out of the way and let us fight it out properly. He saw there was no means of stopping us, and stepped back. García was already hunched like a cat ready to pounce on a mouse. He held his hat in his left hand to ward off blows, and his knife well forward. That's the Andalusian defence they use. But I took up the Navarrese posture, directly opposite him, my left arm raised, my left foot forward, my knife lying along my right thigh. I felt stronger than a giant. He flung himself at me, fast as an arrow – I turned on my left foot, and he encountered thin air, but I stabbed him in the throat, and the knife plunged in so deeply that my hand was under his chin. I twisted the blade so strongly that it snapped. It was all over. The blade shot out of the wound, forced out by a great spurt of bubbling blood as thick as an arm. He fell flat on his face, stiff as a post.

"What have you done?" said El Dancaire.

"Listen," I told him. "There wasn't room for the two of us. I love Carmen, and I want to be the only man in her life. Anyway, García was a real rogue, and I remember what he did to poor Remendado. Now there's just the two of us left, but we're good lads. Look, d'you want me as a friend, till the very end?"

El Dancaire held out his hand to me. He was a man of about fifty.

"Screw all that stupid lovey-dovey nonsense!" he exclaimed. "If you'd asked him for Carmen, he'd have sold her to you for a piastre. Now there's only two of us, how are we going to manage tomorrow?"

"Leave it to me," I replied. "I don't give a damn about anything any more."

We buried García, and went to set up camp two hundred yards further on. The next day, Carmen and her Englishman came by with two muleteers and a servant. I told El Dancaire, "I'll look after the Englishman. You put the wind up the others – they're unarmed."

The Englishman had guts. If Carmen hadn't pushed his arm, he'd have killed me. To cut a long story short, I won Carmen back that day, and my first words were to tell her she was a widow. When she found out how it had happened, she said, "You'll always be a *lillipendi*!* García should have killed you by rights. That Navarrese defence of yours, it's a joke: he's knocked off better fighters than you. His time had come, that's all. So will yours."

"And so will yours too," I replied, "if you're not a true *romi* to me."

"Too right!" she said. "I've seen more than once from the coffee grounds that we were going to end up together. Pah! *Que será, será*."

And she clicked her castanets, as she always did when she wanted to chase away a troublesome thought.

You forget where you are when you start talking about yourself. I'm sure you're bored by all these details, but I'll soon be finished. The life we were leading lasted quite a while. El Dancaire and I had picked up a few mates a bit more reliable than the first lot, and we kept ourselves busy with a spot of smuggling – and, I've got to admit, from time to time we'd do a highway robbery or two, but only as a last resort, and when we had no other choice. In any case, we didn't give the travellers too much grief, and only ever took their money. For a few months, I was quite content with Carmen: she continued to be useful for our operations – she'd alert us to some plum jobs we could carry off. She hung out either in Málaga or Córdoba or Granada, but at a word from me, she'd drop everything and come to find me in some isolated *venta*, or even in the place where we were bivouacking. Only once, in Málaga it was, did she give me any reason for anxiety. I learnt she'd set her cap at a really wealthy merchant, and she was probably planning on trying her hand at another bit of funny business like in Gibraltar. In spite of everything El Dancaire said to stop me, I headed off, and entered Málaga in broad daylight. I looked for Carmen, and I immediately dragged her away. We had an almighty row.

"Do you know," she told me, "that ever since you've been my official *rom*, I love you less than I did when you were my *minchorrò*? I don't want to be hassled, and above all I don't want anyone giving me orders. What I want is to be free and do as I like. Just watch you don't push me too far. If you start bugging me, I'll find some nice young lad who'll treat you the way you treated One-Eye."

El Dancaire patched it up between us, but we'd said things to each other that weighed on our hearts, and we weren't the same as we'd been before. Shortly after that, we had a bit of bad luck. We were surprised by the troops. El Dancaire was killed, as well as two of my mates; two others were captured. I was seriously wounded, and, if it hadn't been for my fine horse, I'd have ended up in the hands of the soldiers. I was completely exhausted, and I had a bullet in me. I went to hole up in a wood with the only mate I still had. I fainted as I tried to get off my horse, and thought I was going to snuff it in the undergrowth, like a hare that's been filled full of lead. My mate dragged me over to a cave we happened to know, then he went to find Carmen. She was in Granada, and she came rushing over straight away. For a whole fortnight she didn't leave my side for an instant. She didn't get a moment's sleep; she looked after me with the kind of care and skill that no other woman ever had, not for even the best-loved of men. As soon as I could stand on my own two feet, she took me to Granada, in total secrecy. *Gitanas* can always find safe refuges, and I spent more than six weeks in a house that was only two doors down from the *corregidor* who was trying to track me down. More than once, peeping out from behind a shutter, I saw him going by. Finally I recovered, but I'd been thinking a lot as I lay on my sickbed, and I was planning to change the way I lived. I talked to Carmen about leaving Spain, and trying to lead an honest life in the New World. She laughed in my face.

"We're not the kind of people that go around planting cabbages," she said. "*Our* destiny is to live off the *payllos*.

Look, I've come to an arrangement with Nathan Ben-Joseph of Gibraltar. He knows you're alive. He's counting on you. What would our colleagues in Gibraltar say if you broke your word to them?"

I gave in to her arguments, and went back to my criminal ways.

While I was hiding out in Gibraltar, there were some bullfights that Carmen went to see. When she got back, she started talking about a very nifty picador named Lucas. She knew his horse's name, and how much his embroidered jacket had cost. I paid no attention. Juanito, the one mate I still had left, told me a few days later that he'd seen Carmen with Lucas in a shop in Zacatín.* Now I started to get worried. I asked Carmen how and why she'd struck up an acquaintance with this picador.

"He's a lad you can do business with," she said. "A river that makes a noise must have water or pebbles in it.* He's won twelve hundred reales at the bullfights. So either we need to get hold of that money, or, as he's a fine horseman and a strong young lad with guts, we can enrol him into our gang. Those two mates of yours got killed – you need replacements. Take him with you."

"I don't want his money or his company," I replied, "and I forbid you to talk to him."

"Watch it!" she said. "Whenever someone tries to stop me doing anything, I just go off and do it that minute!"

Luckily, the picador set off for Málaga, and I got back to the business I'd taken on, smuggling in the Jew's cotton fabrics. That little expedition kept me pretty busy – Carmen too – and I forgot all about Lucas. Perhaps she forgot about him too – at least for the time being. It was round about then, sir, that I met you, first near Montilla, then later on in Córdoba. I won't remind you of our last interview. Maybe you know more about it than I do. Carmen stole your watch – she wanted your money too, especially that ring I can see on your finger... she said it was a magic ring that she just had to have. We had a violent quarrel, and I hit her. She went pale, and started crying. It was the first time I'd seen her crying, and it really upset me. I asked her to forgive me, but she pulled a long face for a whole day, and when I set off for Montilla again, she refused to kiss me goodbye.

I was feeling pretty gloomy when, three days later, she came for me, laughing away and as merry as a skylark. Everything was forgotten, and we went around looking like a couple who'd only just fallen in love. When the time came to separate, she said, "There's a festival on in Córdoba – I'm going to see it, then I'll know which people are heading away loaded with money, and I can tip you off."

I let her leave. When I was alone, I thought about this festival and Carmen's change of mood. "She must have taken her revenge on me already," I said to myself, "since she was the first one to make up."

A peasant told me there were going to be bullfights in Córdoba. This made my blood boil, and I rushed off like a madman straight to the arena. They pointed out Lucas to me, and on the front seats near the barrier I recognized Carmen. I only needed to look at her for a moment to be sure I was right. When Lucas was on his first bull, he started playing the great lover, just as I'd foreseen. He tore off the bull's cockade* and carried it over to Carmen, who placed it in her hair there and then. The bull kindly decided to avenge me. Lucas got knocked over, and ended up with his horse on top of his chest and the bull on top of them both. I looked over at Carmen, but she wasn't in her seat. It was impossible for me to leave mine, and I was obliged to wait for the end of the session. So I went to the house you know, and I lay low all evening and part of the night. Around two in the morning, Carmen returned, and was a bit taken aback to see me there.

"Come with me," I said.

"Fine," she replied, "let's go!"

I went to get my horse – I put her behind the saddle, and we trotted along the whole of the rest of the night without saying a single word to each other. We stopped at daybreak in an isolated *venta*, not very far from a small hermitage. Here I said to Carmen:

"Listen, I'll forget everything. I won't say a word about it to you – just swear to me one thing: you're going to follow me to America, and once we're there, you're going to behave yourself."

"No," she said sulkily, "I don't want to go to America. I'm happy here."

"That's because you can be near Lucas – but just think about it. If he gets better, he's still not going to make old bones. Anyway, why should I take it out on *him*? I'm tired of killing your lovers – you're the one I'm going to kill."

She stared at me with her savage eyes and then said:

"I've always thought you'd kill me. The first time I saw you, I'd just bumped into a priest at the door of my house. And last night, when we left Córdoba, didn't you spot anything? A hare crossed the road between the hooves of your horse. It is written."

"Carmencita," I asked her, "don't you love me any more?"

She didn't reply. She was sitting cross-legged on a mat and drawing lines in the ground with her finger.

"Let's lead a different kind of life, Carmen," I implored her. "Let's go and live somewhere where we will never be separated. You know that, not far from here, we have a hundred and twenty ounces of gold buried under an oak tree... And then we've still got some funds at the Jew's, at Ben-Joseph's."

She started to smile, and said:

"Me first, then you. I know that's how it's got to happen."

"Think it over," I continued. "My patience and my courage are at an end. You make your choice, or I'll make mine."

I left her and went for a walk near the hermitage. I found the hermit saying his prayers. I waited for him to finish praying.

I would dearly have liked to be able to pray, but I couldn't. When he got up again, I went over to him.

"Father," I said to him, "will you pray for someone who is in great peril?"

"I pray for all the afflicted," he said.

"Can you say a mass for a soul that will soon, perhaps, be standing before its maker?"

"Yes," he said, gazing at me.

And, as there was something strange about my appearance, he tried to get me talking.

"I'm sure I've seen you somewhere before," he said.

I placed a piastre on his pew.

"When will you be saying mass?" I asked him.

"In half an hour. The son of the man who runs the inn down there is coming to assist. Tell me, young man, do you have something on your conscience that's tormenting you? Will you listen to the advice of a Christian?"

I felt on the verge of tears. I told him I'd be back, and I fled. I went to lie down on the grass until I heard the bell. Then I walked back, but I stayed outside the chapel. When the mass had been said, I returned to the *venta*. I almost hoped that Carmen had made good her escape – she might have taken my horse and got away... But she was still there. She didn't want anyone to say I'd scared her. During my absence, she'd undone the hem of her dress to get the lead weights out of it. Now she was sitting at a table, gazing into an earthenware bowl full of water, into which she had dropped some lead she'd just melted. She was so preoccupied with her magic that at first she didn't notice my return. One minute she would pick up a piece of lead and turn it this way and that, looking sad, the next she would sing one of those magical songs, calling on María Padilla, the mistress of Don Pedro – she was, they say, the *Bari Crallisa*, or the Great Queen of the *gitanos*.*

"Carmen," I said to her, "will you come with me?"

She stood up, threw down her begging bowl and placed her mantilla over her head as if she were ready to go. They brought me my horse – she climbed up behind me, and off we went.

"So," I said when we had travelled some distance, "my Carmen, you're coming with me, right?"

"I'll follow you to the bitter end, yes, but I won't live with you."

We were in a solitary ravine. I halted my horse.

"Is it here?" she said, and leapt to the ground. She took off her mantilla, threw it to her feet and stood there motionless, hand on hip, gazing at me fixedly.

"You want to kill me, I can see it," she said. "It is written – but you won't make me give in."

"Please, I beg you, be reasonable," I said. "Listen to me! The past is all forgotten. But as you well know, it was you who caused my ruin: for you I became a thief and murderer. Carmen! My Carmen! Let me save you and save myself with you."

"José," she replied, "you're asking me for the impossible. I don't love you any more. You still love me, and that's why you want to kill me. I could easily still lie to you, but I really can't be bothered. It's all over between us. You're my *rom*, and as such you have the right to kill your *romi* – but Carmen will always be free. *Calli* she was born and *calli* she will die."

"So you love Lucas?" I asked her.

"Yes, I loved him, like I did you, for a while – less than you, perhaps. Right now I don't love anything, and I hate myself for having loved you."

I threw myself down at her feet, I grasped her hands, I shed wet tears on them. I reminded her of all the moments of happiness we had enjoyed together. I offered to remain a bandit to please her. Everything, sir, everything! I offered her everything, if only she would love me again!

She told me, "To love you again is out of the question. As for living with you, I don't want to."

I was overwhelmed by fury. I drew my knife. I'd have been glad if she'd shown fear and begged me for mercy, but that woman was a demon.

"For the last time," I cried, "will you stay with me?"

"No! No! No!" she said, stamping on the ground and drawing from her finger a ring I'd given her, which she hurled into the undergrowth.

I struck her twice. It was One-Eye's knife that I'd picked up when I broke mine. She fell at the second blow, without uttering a cry. I can still remember, as if it were now, her big black eyes gazing fixedly at me – then they clouded over and closed. I stayed by her corpse, completely numb, for a good hour. Then I remembered that Carmen had often told me she would like to be buried in a wood. I dug a grave for her with my knife, and laid her in it. I spent a long time looking for her ring, and finally found it. I placed it in the grave with her body, and a little cross too. Perhaps I shouldn't have. Then I climbed onto my horse, galloped to Córdoba and handed myself in at the first guardhouse. I said I'd killed Carmen, but I refused to say where her body was. The hermit was a holy man. He prayed for her! He said a mass for her soul... Poor child! It's the fault of the *Calé* for having brought her up like that.*

IV

Spain is one of the countries where these days, and in even greater numbers than elsewhere, are to be found those nomads scattered across the whole of Europe and known under the name of *Bohémiens*, *Gitanos*, *Gypsies*, *Zigeuner*, etc. Most of them live, or rather lead, a nomadic existence in the provinces of the south and east, in Andalusia, Estremadura and the Kingdom of Murcia; there are many of them in Catalonia. The latter often cross over into France. You come across them at all the fairs in the south of the country. Usually, the men earn a living as horse dealers, vets and mule clippers; they are also skilled at mending big saucepans and copperware, to say nothing of their smuggling and other illicit activities. The women tell fortunes, beg and sell all sorts of drugs, both harmless and otherwise.

The physical characteristics of the Roma are easier to distinguish than to describe, and once you've seen one, you can easily recognize one of their race from among a thousand. Their physiognomy, their expression – this is what mainly separates them from the local settled populations. Their complexion is very suntanned, always much swarthier than that of the other races among which they live. Hence the name of *Calé*, the "blacks", by which they often refer to themselves.* Their eyes look slanted, wide, very dark, with long, luxuriant eyelashes. The expression in them can only be compared to that of a wild beast. Boldness and timidity can be read in them in equal measure, and in this respect their eyes are quite a good guide to the character of the whole nation – crafty, daring, but, like Panurge, *naturally afraid of copping it in the neck.*＊ In general, the men are well proportioned, slim and agile. I don't think I've ever seen one who was on the plump side. In Germany, the Roma women are often very pretty, but beauty is really quite rare among the *gitanas* of Spain. While still young, they can pass muster as likeable Plain Janes, but once they have become mothers, they turn repulsive. Both sexes are incredibly dirty, and unless you've seen the hair of a *gitana* matron you won't easily be able to imagine it, even if you picture the roughest, greasiest, dustiest horsehair. In some of the cities of Andalusia, a few of the young girls, a bit nicer than the others, take slightly more care over their appearance. These ones dance for money – dances that closely resemble those that are forbidden in our public balls at carnival time. Mr Borrow, the English missionary, and the author of two extremely interesting works on the *gitanos* of Spain – whom he had undertaken to convert, being funded by the Bible Society – assures his readers that it has never happened that a *gitana* ever felt the least bit drawn to a man foreign to her race. I think there is a great deal of exaggeration in the praise he lavishes on their chastity. To begin with, most of them are in the same category as the ugly woman in Ovid: *Casta quem nemo rogavit.** As for the pretty ones, they are like all Spanish women: picky when it comes to choosing their lovers. You have to please them – you have to live up to them. Mr Borrow quotes as proof of their virtue a characteristic which does honour to his own sense of virtue, and even more to his naivety. A scoundrelly fellow he knew offered several ounces of gold to a pretty *gitana*, but didn't get what he wanted. An Andalusian man to whom I recounted this anecdote claimed that this scoundrel would have met with more success if he had showed her two or three piastres: to offer ounces of gold to a *gitana* was just as ineffectual a way of persuading her as promising a million or two to an innkeeper's daughter.

Whatever the truth of the matter, it is a certain fact that *gitanas* are extraordinarily devoted to their husbands. There are no dangers or hardships that they will not confront in order to help them in cases of need. One of the names the *gitanos* give themselves, *Romé*, or "the spouses", seems to me to attest to the respect in which their race holds marriage. In general, one can say that their main virtue is patriotism, if that is the right term for the loyalty they observe in their relations with individuals of the same origin as themselves, their zeal to come to each other's help and the inviolable secrecy they maintain in potentially compromising matters. In fact, we find a similar state of affairs in all mysterious and outlawed associations.

A few months ago, I visited a band of Roma living in the Vosges. In the hut of an old woman, the elder of the tribe, there was a Roma from a different family who was suffering from a deadly illness. This man had left a hospital where he was being well looked after to go and die amidst his compatriots. For thirteen weeks he had been bedridden at his hosts', and much better treated than the sons and sons-in-law who lived in the same house. He had a nice bed of straw and moss, with reasonably clean sheets, while the rest of the family, eleven all told, slept on planks three feet long. This is how great their hospitality is. The same woman, so humane towards her guest, kept saying to me right in front of the sick man, "*Singo, singo, homte hi mulo*" ("Soon, soon, he'll have to die"). After all, the lives of these people are so wretched that they are in no way alarmed to hear that death is imminent.

One remarkable characteristic of the Roma is their indifference when it comes to religion – not that they are freethinkers or sceptics. They have never professed atheism. Far from it – the religion of the country they live in is the one they take as their own: they simply change it each time they change country. The superstitions which replace religious feelings among uncultivated people are equally foreign to them. How, after all, could superstitions exist among people who, as often as not, live off the credulity of others? However, I have noticed that Spanish *gitanos* have a remarkable and powerful aversion to any contact with a corpse. Few of them would consent to bear a body to the cemetery even for money.

I have said that most Romani women were involved in fortune-telling. They do it really quite well. But what for them is a real source of profit is the sale of charms and love potions. Not only do they have a provision of toads' legs to keep fickle affections in their place and powdered lodestone so you can gain the love of a cold-hearted person: they will even, if need be, cast powerful spells that can force the Devil to come to their aid. Last year, a Spanish woman told me the following story. She was walking along the Alcalá Street, downcast and anxious. A *gitana* squatting on the pavement called out to her, "My fair lady, your lover has betrayed you."

This was quite true.

"Do you want me to win him back for you?"

It is easy to understand how joyfully the proposition was accepted, and how great must have been the trust inspired by a person who could thus guess, at a glance, the heart's innermost secrets. Since it would have been impossible to proceed to any magical operations in the busiest street in Madrid, they agreed to meet the next day.

"There's nothing easier than to get the faithless man falling back at your feet," said the *gitana*. "Would you by any chance have a handkerchief, a scarf or a mantilla he's given you?"

A silk shawl was handed over.

"Now take some crimson thread and sew a piastre into one corner of the shawl. In another corner sew a half-piastre; here, a small coin; there, a two-real piece. Then you have to sew a gold coin into the middle. A doubloon would be best."

The doubloon and the rest were all sewn in.

"Now give me the shawl, I'll take it to the *campo santo*,* on the stroke of midnight. Come with me, if you want to see a nice bit of devilry. I promise you that tomorrow you'll see the man you love."

The *gitana* set off alone for the *campo santo*, since the other woman was too scared of devils to go with her. I leave you to guess whether the poor abandoned woman ever saw her shawl or her faithless lover again.

Despite their poverty and the kind of aversion they inspire, Roma nonetheless enjoy a certain esteem among people who don't know any better, and they are very vain of the fact. They feel that they are a superior race when it comes to intelligence, and they cordially despise the populace that grants them hospitality.

"The gentiles are so stupid," a Roma woman from the Vosges told me, "that there's no great merit in catching them out. The other day, a peasant woman called out to me on the street. I went into her house. Her stove was smoking, and she asked me to cast a spell to make it go away. First I make sure she gives me a nice piece of bacon. Then I start mumbling a few words in Romani.

'You're stupid,' I said. 'You were born a fool, and you'll die a fool.' When I was at the door, I told her in good German, 'An infallible way of making sure your stove doesn't smoke is not to light a fire under it.' And I took to my heels."

The history of the Roma is still problematic. It is known for a fact that the first bands of them, very small in number, appeared in the east of Europe near the beginning of the fifteenth century, but no one can say where they came from, nor why they arrived in Europe – and, what is much more extraordinary, nobody knows how they managed to increase in number so dramatically in such a short time, and in several different and widely separated countries. The Roma themselves have preserved no tradition of their origins, and if most of them name Egypt as their primitive homeland, this is because they have adopted a fable about them that was already widespread long ago.

Most orientalists who have studied the Roma language think that they originated in India. And a great number of the roots and grammatical forms of Romani are indeed found in the languages derived from Sanskrit. It is highly conceivable that, in their long wanderings, the Roma adopted many foreign words. In all the dialects of Romani, you find a number of Greek words. For example, *cocal*, bone, from κόκκαλον; *petali*, a horseshoe, from πέταλον; *cafi*, nail, from καρφί, etc. These days the Roma have almost as many different dialects as there are different, separate bands of their race. Everywhere, they speak the language of the country they live in more easily than their own language, which they hardly make use of except when they want to speak to each other unconstrained by the presence of strangers. If you compare the dialect of German Roma with that of the Spanish, who have been out of touch with the former for centuries, you will recognize a great number of words in common, but the original language has everywhere been noticeably affected, albeit to different degrees, by the contact of more cultivated languages which these nomads have been obliged to use. German on the one hand, and Spanish on the other, have so modified the basis of Romani that it would be impossible for a Roma from the Black Forest to converse with one of his Andalusian brothers, even though they need only to exchange a few sentences to recognize that they are both speaking a dialect derived from the same language. Some very frequently used words are, I believe, common to all dialects. Thus, in all the vocabularies I have been able to examine, *pani* means "water"; *manro*, "bread", *mâs*, "meat"; and *lon*, "salt".

The names of numerals are pretty much the same everywhere. The German dialect seems to me much purer than the Spanish dialect, as it has preserved several primitive grammatical forms, whereas the *gitanos* have adopted those of Castilian. However, there are a few words which form an exception and attest to the ancient shared origin of the languages.

The preterites of the German dialect are formed by adding *ium* to the imperative, which is always the root of the verb. The verbs in Spanish Romani are all conjugated on the model of Castilian first-conjugation verbs. From the infinitive *jamar*, "to eat", we should be able to form *jamé*, "I have eaten"; from *lillar*, "to take", we should be able to form *lillé*, "I have taken". However, some old *gitanos* say, by way of exception: "*jayon*", "*lillon*". I don't know of any other verbs which have preserved this ancient form.

While I am thus parading my somewhat slender knowledge of the Romani language, I must note a few words of French slang that our thieves have stolen from the Roma. From *The Mysteries of Paris*,* law-abiding people have learnt that *chourin* meant "knife". This is pure Romani: *tchouri* is one of the words common to all the dialects I have mentioned. Monsieur Vidocq* calls a horse *grés*, another Roma word: *gras*, *gre*, *graste*, *gris*. Then there's the word *romanichel*, which, in Parisian slang, designates the Roma. This is a corrupt form of *romané tchave*, "Roma lads". But an etymology of which I am rather proud is that of *frimousse*, "expression" or "face", a word that all schoolboys use, or at least did in my day. Observe, to begin with, that Oudin, in his curious dictionary (1640),* wrote *firlimousse*. Now, *firla*, *fila*, in Romani means face, and *mui* has the same meaning: it is exactly the same word as *os* in Latin. The combination *firlamui* was immediately understood by a purist Roma speaker, and I believe it conforms to the genius of his language.*

This is more than enough to give the readers of 'Carmen' a flattering idea of my studies on Romani. I will end with this proverb, which seems entirely appropriate: *En retudi panda nasti abela macha* – "Keep your mouth shut, and you'll keep the flies out".

THE VENUS OF ILLE

Ἵλεως, ἦν δ᾽ἐγώ, ἔστω ὁ ἀνδριὰς καὶ ἤπιος οὕτως ἀνδρεῖος ὤν.
ΛΟΥΚΙΑΝΟΥ ΦΙΛΟΨΕΥΔΗΣ*

I was walking down the last slope of the Canigou, and, even though the sun had already set, I could make out in the plain the houses of the small town of Ille,* to which I was heading.

"I suppose you know," I said to the Catalan who had been acting as my guide since the previous day, "where Monsieur de Peyrehorade lives?"

"Do I know where he lives!…" he exclaimed. "I know his house as well as my own – and if it wasn't so dark, I'd point it out to you. It's the finest house in Ille. He's a wealthy man, is Monsieur de Peyrehorade, oh yes – and he's marrying off his son into the family of an even wealthier man than himself."

"And is the wedding going to happen soon?" I asked.

"Very soon! The violinists might well already have been booked for the party. This evening, perhaps… tomorrow, or the day after – I don't know! It'll be in Puygarrig: it's Mademoiselle de Puygarrig that the son's marrying. It'll be a great occasion, oh yes!"

I'd been recommended to M. de Peyrehorade by my friend M. de P—. I'd been told he was a very learned antiquarian, and his willingness to help knew no bounds. He would count it a real pleasure to show me all the ruins for ten leagues around. Now, I was relying on him to visit the environs of Ille: I knew there were many ancient and medieval monuments in this area. This marriage, which I had not heard about until then, threatened to put out all my plans.

"I'm going to be in the way," I said to myself. Still, I *was* expected: since M. de P— had told them I was coming, I would have to introduce myself.

"Let's make a bet, Monsieur," my guide told me, once we were down on the plain. "Shall we bet a cigar that I can guess what you're going to do at Monsieur de Peyrehorade's?"

"Yes, but that's not particularly difficult to guess," I replied, handing him a cigar. "At this time of day, when you've walked six leagues across the Canigou, the first item on the agenda is supper."

"Yes, but what about tomorrow?… Look, I bet you're coming to Ille to see the idol? I guessed as much when I saw you drawing the portraits of the saints in Serrabone."*

"The idol? What idol?" This word had aroused my curiosity.

"What? You mean they didn't tell you in Perpignan about how Monsieur de Peyrehorade had found an idol buried in the ground?"

"You mean a terracotta statue, one made out of clay?"

"No, no. Actually it was made out of copper – big enough to be pretty valuable. It weighs as much as a church bell. It was right deep down in the ground, at the foot of an olive tree – that's where we found it."

"So you were there when it was discovered?"

"Yes, Monsieur. Monsieur de Peyrehorade told us a fortnight ago – Jean Coll and me, that is – to dig up an old olive tree that had got frozen to death last winter… you remember what a hard winter it was. So while he was digging away for all he was worth, Jean Coll stuck his pickaxe in and I hear a 'bong!'… just like he'd struck against a bell. 'What's all this?' I says to myself. We keep on digging away, and suddenly what do we see but a black hand looking like the hand of a dead man sticking up out of the ground. I was in a right funk. I go up to Monsieur, and I says to him, 'There's some dead bodies, master, out there under the olive tree! Better call for the priest.'

"'What dead bodies?' he says to me. He comes over, and no sooner has he seen the hand than he shouts, 'An antique! An antique!' You'd have thought he'd found some treasure. And soon he was digging away like fury, with the pickaxe, with his bare hands even, and working almost as hard as the other two of us put together."

"So what did you find, then?"

"A big black woman, more than half bare she was, saving Your Reverence, Monsieur, all in copper, and Monsieur de Peyrehorade told us as she was an idol from pagan times... from Charlemagne's day, no less!"

"I know what it is... A fine example of a Blessed Virgin in bronze, from a ruined convent."

"A Blessed Virgin, was it now?... I'd have recognized it if it'd been a Blessed Virgin. It's an idol, I tell you – you can tell from the way she looks. She fixes her big white eyes on you... You feel like she's staring straight at you. You have to lower your eyes, you do, when you look at her."

"White eyes? Surely they're encrusted in bronze... It's most likely some Roman statue."

"Roman! That's right! Monsieur de Peyrehorade told me as she's a Roman lady. Ah, I can see you're a real scholar like him."

"Is she all in one piece, well preserved?"

"Oh yes, Monsieur! There's nothing missing. It's even more beautiful and nicely worked than the bust of Louis-Philippe,* the one in the town hall, in painted plaster. Still, for all that, I can't really take a liking to that there idol's face. She looks vicious to me... and she *is* vicious, too."

"Vicious? What's she done to make you call her 'vicious'?"

"Not exactly to me – but you'll see. Four of us had got together to pull her upright, and Monsieur de Peyrehorade too, he was pulling on the rope too, even though he don't have much more strength than a chicken, fine gentleman that he is! We pull and we pull and at last she's upright. I was just a-reachin' down to pick up a bit of broken tile to wedge her up when crash, bang, wallop! Blow me if she don't come toppling over backwards. I says: 'Watch out!' But not quick enough. Jean Coll didn't have time to pull his leg out of the way…"

"So was he wounded?"

"Snapped as clean as a vine prop, his poor leg. Damn me! When I saw that, I was bloody furious, I can tell you. I wanted to hack that idol to pieces with my pickaxe, but Monsieur de Peyrehorade held me back. He gave some money to Jean Coll, though to tell you the truth he's still in bed, even though it was a fortnight ago that it happened to him, and the doctor says as he'll never walk on that leg as well as he does on the other. It's a shame, too, him as was our best runner and, after the young master, the niftiest pelota player there could be. Monsieur Alphonse de Peyrehorade was really down in the mouth about it, as it was Coll, who used to play with him. A fine sight it was, too, when they hit the balls back to each other. Thwock! Thwock! Those balls never even touched the ground."

Still chatting, we came into Ille, and I found myself standing before M. de Peyrehorade. He was a short elderly fellow, still in his prime, as dapper as they come, with his powdered wig, his red nose, his jovial and roguish manner. Before he'd even opened M. de P—'s letter, he'd sat me down in front of a splendid meal and introduced me to his wife and his son as a distinguished archaeologist who was going to rescue Roussillon from the oblivion to which it had been relegated by the indifference of the scholarly world.

As I heartily fell to (after all, nothing sharpens your appetite more than the fresh mountain air), I examined my hosts. I've said a few words about M. de Peyrehorade. I must add that he was the liveliest figure you could imagine. He would talk, eat, rise to his feet, run over to his library, bring back books for me, show me engravings, top up my glass – he couldn't sit still for two minutes. His wife, a bit too much on the plump side, like most Catalan women the wrong side of forty, struck me as a thoroughly provincial woman, entirely preoccupied by looking after her household. Although the supper was more than enough for at least six people, she scurried over to the kitchen, ordered them to kill some pigeons and fry up some *miliasses*,* and opened I don't know how many jars of jam. In a moment, the table was groaning under dishes and bottles, and I'd have certainly died of indigestion even if I'd only as much as tasted everything I was offered. Still, every time I turned down a dish, they found some new excuse. They were afraid I might find myself very inadequately catered for in Ille. Out in the provinces, people have so few resources, and Parisians are so picky!

In the midst of his parents' comings and goings, M. Alphonse de Peyrehorade didn't move more than if he'd been a Roman boundary statue. He was a tall young man, twenty-six years old, with a handsome, well-proportioned face, if somewhat lacking in expression. His slimness and his athletic figure justified perfectly the local reputation he had as a tireless pelota player. On this particular evening, he was dressed with great elegance, and his costume was clearly copied from an engraving in the latest *Journal des modes*.* But he seemed to be uncomfortable in his clothes: he was as stiff as a ramrod in his velvet collar, and could only turn round if he moved his whole upper body. His rough, weather-beaten hands and his short fingernails contrasted remarkably with his costume. They were a farm labourer's hands emerging from the cuffs of a dandy. Furthermore, even if he did look me up and down from head to toe with great curiosity, as I was a Parisian, he only once spoke to me in the course of the whole evening, and this was to ask me where I'd bought my watch chain.

"Ah, my dear fellow!" said M. de Peyrehorade to me as the supper drew to its close. "You're my guest – you're all mine now that you're in my house! I won't let go of you until you've seen all the places of interest in our mountains. You really must get to know this Roussillon of ours, and give it its due. You have no idea of all the things we're going to show you. Monuments from every age – Phoenician, Celtic, Roman, Arabic, Byzantine: you'll see everything, from the cedar tree even unto the hyssop. I'm going to take you everywhere, and I'll not allow you to neglect a single brick."

A fit of coughing made him break off. I took advantage of the interruption to tell him that I would be most sorry to be a nuisance at a time of such excitement for his family. If he would be so good as to give me his excellent advice on the excursions I would be undertaking, I could then, without causing him the bother of accompanying me—

"Ha! You mean the wedding of that young fellow over there!" he exclaimed, interrupting me. "A mere trifle! It's happening the day after tomorrow. You can come and celebrate with us: it's just a family get-together – the fiancée is in mourning... she's lost an aunt and gained her inheritance. So there won't be a party, and no dancing... It's a shame... you'd have seen our Catalan girls dancing... They're pretty, and you might well have been inspired to imitate young Alphonse. One wedding, they say, leads to another... On Saturday, once the young couple have been married, I'll be free, and we can set off. I must apologize for forcing you to endure a provincial wedding. For a Parisian who's seen more parties than he can remember... and a wedding without any dancing, on top of that! Still, you'll be seeing a bride... a bride... well, you can tell me what you think... Anyway, you're a serious kind of a chap... you don't have much of an eye for women any more. I've got better things than that to show you. I've got something really good for you to see!... I'm keeping a nice little surprise in reserve for tomorrow."

"Good Heavens!" I told him. "It's difficult to keep any piece of treasure in one's home without the public finding out about it. I think I can guess the surprise you're saving up for me. But if it's your statue you're talking about, the description my guide has given me has only whetted my curiosity and made me all too ready to pay my homage."

"Ah! He's told you about the 'idol' – that's what they call my lovely Venus Tur— But I won't say any more about it. Tomorrow, in broad daylight, you'll see her, and then you can tell me whether

I'm right to think she's a masterpiece. Good Lord, yes – you couldn't have come at a better time! There are some inscriptions that I interpret the best I can. But I'm a bit of an ignoramus, and you're… a scholar from Paris!… Perhaps you'll laugh at my translation… I've written an article, you know… yes, yours truly has written… old provincial antiquarian that I am, I've launched into… I'm going to make the printing presses groan!… If you'd be so kind as to read my stuff and correct it, I might have a chance of… For instance, I'm really curious to know how you'd translate this inscription on the base: CAVE— But now's not the time to ask! Let's leave it until tomorrow, eh? Tomorrow! Not a word about the Venus today!"

"You're right, Peyrehorade, to drop your idol for now," said his wife. "You ought to have realized you're stopping Monsieur from eating. Monsieur has seen much finer statues than yours in Paris, you know. In the Tuileries, there are dozens of them – bronze ones, too!"

"Ah, what a fine example of the sheer ignorance, the *sancta simplicitas** of the provinces!" M. de Peyrehorade interrupted her. "Comparing an admirable antique with Coustou's insipid figures!* *My housewife speaks of gods without due reverence.** Did you know that my wife wanted me to melt down my statue to turn it into a bell for our church? Then she'd have been able to stand sponsor to it. A masterpiece by Myro,* Monsieur!"

"Masterpiece, masterpiece!… A fine masterpiece *she* is! Breaking a man's leg!"

"Look, m'dear, d'you see this?" said M. de Peyrehorade resolutely, thrusting out towards her his right leg in a silk chiné stocking. "If my Venus had broken this very leg, I would be happy to live without it!"

"Good God! Peyrehorade, how can you *say* that? It's a good thing the poor man is getting better… All the same, I still can't bring myself to even look at a statue that can cause nasty accidents like that. Poor Jean Coll!"

"Wounded by Venus, Monsieur," said M. de Peyrehorade, with a coarse laugh, "wounded by Venus, and the rascal dares complain!

*Veneris nec præmia noris.**

Who has never been wounded by Venus?"

Monsieur Alphonse, who understood French better than Latin, winked with a conniving expression, and glanced at me as if to ask, "What about you, Parisian – d'you get it?"

The supper ended. I had stopped eating an hour ago. I was tired, and I couldn't disguise the frequent yawns that kept escaping from my lips. Mme de Peyrehorade was the first to notice, and remarked that it was time to get some sleep. This was the cue for a new round of excuses about the poor lodgings I would be forced to endure. I wouldn't be as comfortable as in Paris. In the provinces, people just have to do the best they can! I would need to be indulgent towards the people of Roussillon. However much I protested that, after a trek through the mountains, a bale of hay would be a perfectly delightful bed, they kept begging me to forgive poor country folk if they couldn't treat me as well as they would have liked. Finally, I made my way up to the bedroom that had been made ready for me, accompanied by M. de Peyrehorade. The staircase, whose higher stairs were of wood, led to the middle of a corridor, off which several bedrooms opened.

"On the right," said my host, "is the apartment I am intending to give to the future Madame Alphonse. Your room is at the end of the opposite corridor. I'm sure you'll agree," he added with what he hoped would seem a knowing expression, "that you have to keep newly-weds away from everyone else. You're at one end of the house, they're at the other."

We went into a well-furnished room, where the first object my eyes fell on was a bed, seven feet long and six feet wide, and so high that you needed a stool to hoist yourself onto it. Once my host had pointed out where the bell for the servants was and assured himself that the sugar basin was full and the little bottles of eau de Cologne duly placed on the dressing table – and once he had asked me several times if I had everything I needed – he wished me a good night and left me.

The windows were closed. Before I got undressed, I opened one of them to breathe in the fresh night air, so very welcome after a long supper. Opposite me was the Canigou, which in every time and season was an admirable sight, but which on that particular evening seemed the most beautiful mountain in the world, illumined as it was by a brilliant moon. I stood gazing at its wonderful outline for a few minutes, and then went to close my window – when, looking down, I noticed the statue on a pedestal some forty yards away from the house. It was placed in the corner of a quickset hedge that separated a small garden from a huge and perfectly smooth rectangular enclosure which was, as I later learnt, the town pelota court. This piece of land, part of M. de Peyrehorade's property, had been given by him to the municipality, at his son's insistent request.

At this distance, it was difficult for me to make out the statue's posture: I could merely guess at its height, which seemed about six feet. Just then, two young scamps from the town sauntered across the pelota court, quite close to the hedge, whistling that fine Roussillon tune, 'Montagnes Régalades'.* They stopped to look at the statue – one of them even heckled it. He was speaking Catalan, but I had been in Roussillon long enough to be able to understand more or less what he was saying.

"Just look at you, you nasty little slut!" (The Catalan term he used was rather stronger.) "Just look at you!" he said. "So it was you that broke Jean Coll's leg! If you belonged to me, I'd break your neck."

"Oh yes? And what with?" said the other. "She's made out of copper, and she's so hard that Étienne broke his file on her when he tried to make a nick in her. It's copper from pagan times – it's harder than anything."

"If I had my cold chisel" (apparently, he was an apprentice locksmith) "I'd soon make her big white eyes pop out, the same way I prise an almond out of its shell. There must be more than a hundred sous' worth of silver in there."

They started to stroll away.

"I just need to wish the idol goodnight," said the bigger of the apprentice boys, suddenly stopping.

He bent down, doubtless to pick up a stone. I saw him flex his arm and throw something, and a loud clang immediately echoed from the bronze. At the same moment the apprentice's hand shot to his head, as he cried out in pain.

"She's hit me back!" he exclaimed.

And those two scamps took to their heels in flight. It was obvious that the stone had rebounded off the metal and had punished that young scoundrel for the outrage he had committed against the goddess.

I closed the window, laughing heartily.

"Another vandal punished by Venus! May all the destroyers of our ancient monuments get a similar headache!" And uttering this charitable desire, I went to sleep.

It was broad daylight when I awoke. Next to my bed were standing, on the one side, M. de Peyrehorade in his dressing gown, and on the other a servant sent by his wife, holding a cup of chocolate.

"Come on, time to get up, Parisian! Ah, these lazy blighters from the capital!" said my host as I hastily got dressed. "It's eight o'clock and he's still in bed! *I've* been up and about since six. I've climbed up here three times – I tiptoed over to your door: nothing, not a sign of life. It won't do you any good, sleeping too much at your age. And you haven't even seen my Venus yet! Come on now, hurry up and drink this cup of Barcelona chocolate... Real contraband stuff... Chocolate of the kind you can't find in Paris. Get your strength up: once you're standing in front of my Venus, there'll be no tearing you away."

In five minutes I was ready – or, rather, I was half-shaven, my buttons all done up wrong and my mouth scorched by the chocolate that I'd swallowed while it was still boiling hot. I went down into the garden, and found myself in front of an admirable statue.

It was indeed a figure of Venus, and a marvellously beautiful one. The upper part of her body was naked, in the way the ancients usually represented their great divinities. Her right hand, lifted to the level of her breast, was turned with the palm facing inwards and the thumb and first two fingers extended, the other two being gently bent. Her left hand, closer to her hip, was holding up the drapery that covered the lower part of her body. The posture of this statue made me think of the pose adopted by the statue of the "Morra Player", generally called, I don't know why, "Germanicus". Perhaps the intention had been to represent the goddess playing morra.*

Be that as it may, nothing more perfect can be imagined than the body of this Venus – nothing smoother and more voluptuous than her outline, nothing more elegant and noble than her drapery. I had been expecting a work from the Late Empire – what I saw was a masterpiece from the great age of statuary. What especially struck me was the exquisite realism of her shape: she seemed to have been cast from a living model, if nature could ever have produced such a perfect form.

Her hair, swept back off her forehead, looked as if it had once been gilded. Her head, small like almost all the heads on Greek statues, was slightly bent forward. As for her face, I will never manage to describe its strange character adequately: in type it was completely different from that of any ancient statue I can remember. It was not the calm, severe beauty created by Greek sculptors, who systematically gave every feature a majestic immobility. Here, on the contrary, I could observe with surprise the artist's explicit intention of creating an expression of malice, and even wickedness. All her features were slightly contracted: her eyes rather slanted, the corners of her mouth twisted up, and her nostrils were flaring somewhat. Disdain, irony and cruelty could be read on this face, which was nonetheless incredibly beautiful. In fact, the more you gazed at this admirable statue, the more you experienced a painful feeling at the way such a marvellous beauty could be combined with the absence of any sensibility.

"If the model ever existed," I said to M. de Peyrehorade, "and I doubt that Heaven has ever produced a woman such as this, how I pity her lovers! She must have taken great pleasure in making them die of despair. There is something ferocious in her expression, and yet I've never seen anything so beautiful."

"*It is Venus entire with her claws in her prey!*"* exclaimed M. de Peyrehorade, satisfied at the enthusiasm I was demonstrating.

This expression of infernal irony was, perhaps, increased by the contrast between her eyes encrusted with silver, shining very brightly, and the blackish-green patina that time had given to the entire statue. These shining eyes produced a certain illusion that evoked life and reality. I remembered what my guide had told me: that she made everyone who looked at her lower their eyes. This was almost true, and I could not restrain a moment of irritation at myself for feeling somewhat ill at ease in front of this bronze figure.

"Now that you've admired everything in detail, my dear colleague in dusty antiquarian studies," said my host, "let's open the proceedings, if you please, of our scholarly conference. What do you have to say about this inscription? You haven't paid any attention to it yet!"

He showed me the plinth on which the statue stood, and I there read these words:

CAVE AMANTEM

"*Quid dicis, doctissime?*"* he asked me, rubbing his hands together. "Let's see if we can come to some agreement about the meaning of this *cave amantem*!"

"But it's got two meanings," I said. "You can translate it as: 'Beware of whoever loves you – don't trust your lovers'. But, if you give it this meaning, I'm not sure if *cave amantem* is really authentic Latin. On looking at the lady's diabolical expression, I'm inclined to think rather that the artist has tried to put the spectator on guard against this terrible beauty. So I'd translate it by 'Beware if *she* loves you'."

"Humph!" said M. de Peyrehorade. "Yes, that's a very worthy meaning. But if you don't mind me saying so, I prefer the first translation, though I'd also like to add a few comments. Do you know who Venus's lovers are?"

"There are several of them."

"Yes, but the first is Vulcan. Wasn't the intended meaning: 'Despite all your beauty and your disdainful air, you'll have a blacksmith – a nasty, coarse, lame fellow, for a lover?' A profound lesson, Monsieur, for flirtatious ladies everywhere!"

I couldn't restrain a smile – his explanation seemed so very far-fetched. "Latin is such a confoundedly *concise* language," I observed, to avoid having to contradict my antiquarian friend too blatantly – and I stepped a few paces back so as to have a better view of the statue.

"One moment, dear colleague!" said M. de Peyrehorade, holding me back by the arm. "You haven't seen everything yet. There's another inscription. Climb up onto the plinth and look at the right arm." As he spoke, he gave me a lift up.

I clung rather unceremoniously to Venus's neck: I was starting to be on familiar terms with her. I looked at her, for a moment, *right in the face*, and from up close I found her even more malevolent and even more beautiful. Then I realized that there were, engraved on her arm, some characters written in an ancient cursive style – or so it seemed to me. Popping on my specs,* I spelt out what follows, and M. de Peyrehorade meanwhile repeated each word as I pronounced it, expressing his approval in voice and gesture. And so I read:

VENERI TVRBVL...
EVTYCHES MYRO
IMPERIO FECIT.

After the word TVRBVL in the first line, I thought I could make out a few letters that had been worn away, but TVRBVL was perfectly readable.

"And *that* means?..." my host asked me, with a beaming and somewhat malicious smile. He knew perfectly well I wouldn't get round TVRBVL that easily.

"There's a word I still don't understand," I told him. "All the rest is easy. Eutyches Myro* made this offering to Venus at her command."

"Absolutely right. But TVRBVL, what are you going to do about that? What's it mean, TVRBVL?"

"TVRBVL has got me stumped. I'm trying to remember an epithet known to have been applied to Venus: that would help me out. But I can't. Maybe... what do you think of TVRBVLENTA? Venus who disturbs, who brings unrest... You'll have noticed that I'm still preoccupied by her malevolent expression. TVRBVLENTA: not a bad epithet to apply to Venus," I added rather tentatively, since I myself was not entirely happy with my explanation.

"Venus the Turbulent! Venus the Troublemaker! Ha! So you think my Venus is the kind of Venus who hangs around in bars? Not at all, Monsieur: she's a Venus with a bit of class. But I'll explain this TVRBVL... You'll at least promise me not to divulge my discovery before my article gets published. You see... well, I'm really proud of this little find... You need to leave us poor provincial devils just a *few* gleanings. You have so much already, you Paris scholars!"

From the top of the pedestal, where I was still perched, I solemnly promised that I would never stoop so low as to steal his discovery from him.

"TVRBVL, Monsieur," he said, coming up to me and lowering his voice in case anyone other than me might overhear him, "is to be read as TVRBVLNERÆ."

"I still don't get it."

"Listen. A league away from here, at the foot of a mountain, there's a village called Boulternère. That's is a corruption of the Latin word TVRBVLNERA. These inversions are extremely common. Boulternère, Monsieur, was once a Roman town. I'd always suspected as much, but I'd never found any proof. And here it is. This Venus was the local deity of the township of Boulternère – and this word Boulternère, which is, as I have just demonstrated, of ancient origin, proves something even more curious: namely, that Boulternère, before being a Roman town, was a Phoenician town!"*

He paused for a moment to catch his breath and enjoy my surprise. I managed to suppress a strong desire to laugh.

"In fact," he continued, "TVRBVLNERA is pure Phoenician: TVR you pronounce TVR... TVR and SUR is the same word – right? SUR is the Phoenician name of Tyre – I don't need to remind you what it means. BVL is Baal – Bâl, Bel, Bul... they're all just slightly different ways of pronouncing it. As for NERA, that's causing me a few problems. I'm tempted to believe, since I can't find a Phoenician word, that it comes from the Greek νηρός, 'damp', 'swampy'. So it must be a hybrid word. To justify νηρός, I'll show you in Boulternère how the mountain streams gather there in foul pools. Also, the ending NERA could have been added much later, in honour of Nera Pivesuvia, the wife of Tetricus, who presumably did a good turn for the town of Turbul.* But because of the pools I mentioned, I prefer the etymology νηρός."

He took a pinch of snuff, looking very pleased with himself.

"But let's forget the Phoenicians, and come back to the inscription. My translation thus goes like this: 'To Venus of Boulternère, Myro dedicates at her command this statue, his work.'"

83

I refrained from criticizing his etymology, but I wanted in my turn to prove my powers of penetration, so I told him, "Hold on a minute, Monsieur. Myro dedicated something, but I don't in the least see why it should be this statue."

"But wasn't Myro a famous Greek sculptor?" he exclaimed. "His talent must have run in his family: it will have been one of his descendants who made this statue. There's absolutely no doubt about it."

"But I can see a little hole on the arm," I replied. "I think it must have been used to fix something on – a bracelet, for instance – that this Myro gave to Venus as an expiatory offering. Myro was a star-crossed lover. Venus was angry with him: he appeased her by dedicating a golden bracelet to her. Remember that *fecit* can often mean the same as *consecravit*. They're synonymous terms. I could show you more than one example if I had Gruter to hand, or Orelli.* It's quite natural for a lover to have a dream vision of Venus, to imagine she's commanding him to give a gold bracelet to her statue. Myro dedicates a bracelet to her... Then the barbarians, or else some sacrilegious robber—"

"Oh, you're just demonstrating your fine talent for storytelling!" exclaimed my host, giving me a hand to help me down. "No, Monsieur, it's a work from the school of Myro. Just look at the workmanship: you're bound to agree."

Since I had sworn never to contradict pig-headed antiquarians too insistently, I lowered my head with a convinced expression and said, "It *is* a marvellous statue."

"Oh my God!" shouted M. de Peyrehorade. "Another piece of vandalism! Somebody's gone and thrown a stone at my statue!"

He had just noticed a white mark slightly above Venus's breast. I spotted a similar trace on the fingers of her right hand. At the time, I supposed they had been grazed as the stone went whizzing by – or else a little piece of it had been chipped off on impact and had ricocheted back onto the hand. I told my host about the outrage that I had witnessed and the prompt punishment that had ensued. This made him laugh loud and long, and, comparing the apprentice boy to Diomedes, he expressed the hope that the lad would, like the Greek hero, see all his companions changed into white birds.*

The bell for lunch interrupted this classical *conversazione*, and, just as on the evening before, I was obliged to eat as much as four men. Then M. de Peyrehorade's farmers turned up – and while he was hearing their reports, his son took me to see an open carriage he had bought for his fiancée in Toulouse, and for which I, of course, voiced my admiration. Then I went into the stables with him, and he kept me there for half an hour, proudly showing off his horses, giving me their genealogies, telling me all the prizes they'd won in the regional races. Eventually, he brought the subject round to his intended, being led to that topic by the grey mare he had set aside for her.

"We'll be seeing her today," he said. "I don't know whether you'll think she's pretty. You're difficult to please in Paris, but everyone, here and in Perpignan, finds her charming. The nice thing is she's very well off. Her aunt in Prades left all her estate to her. Oh! I'm really going to be in clover!"

I was deeply shocked to see a young man seemingly more enthusiastic about the dowry his future wife was bringing him than about her lovely eyes.

"Do you know anything about jewels?" continued M. Alphonse. "What do you think about this one? It's the ring I'm giving her tomorrow."

As he spoke, he drew a big diamond-studded ring in the shape of two interlaced hands from the first joint of his little finger. The allusion struck me as altogether poetic. The workmanship was very old, but I guessed it had been touched up to provide a mounting for the diamonds. Within the ring could be read these words, in Gothic letters:

"*Sempr'ab ti*", meaning "for ever with you".

"It's a lovely ring," I told him. "But those diamonds that have been added mean it's lost something of its character."

"Oh, it's much more beautiful as it is now," he replied with a smile. "There are twelve hundred francs' worth of diamonds here. It was my mother who gave it to me. It was a family ring, very ancient... from the times of chivalry. It had been worn by my grandmother, who'd got it from hers. God knows when it was made."

"The custom in Paris," I said, "is to give a quite simple ring, usually composed of two different metals, such as gold and platinum. Look, that other ring, the one you've got on this finger here, would be just the thing. That big one, with its diamonds and its hands in relief, is so bulky you wouldn't be able to get a glove on over it."

"Oh, that's Madame Alphonse's problem! I still think she'll be glad to have it. Twelve hundred francs' worth on your finger – that's a nice thought. *This* ring," he added, with a self-satisfied look at the smooth little ring he was wearing, "was given me by a woman in Paris, one Mardi Gras. Oh, I certainly lived it up when I was in Paris, two years ago! *That's* the place for a good time!..." And he heaved a sigh of nostalgia.

We had been invited to dinner that evening at Puygarrig, at the home of the bride-to-be. We climbed into the carriage and headed off to the chateau, about a league and a half away from Ille. I was introduced and welcomed as a friend of the family. I won't talk about the dinner or the conversation that followed, in which I took little part. M. Alphonse, who was placed next to his betrothed, said a word in her ear every quarter of an hour. As for her, she hardly ever looked up, and each time her suitor spoke to her, she blushed with modesty, but replied to him without bashfulness.

Mlle de Puygarrig was eighteen; her supple, delicate figure contrasted with the bony angularity of her robust fiancé. She was not only beautiful, but alluring too. I admired the perfect naturalness of all her replies, and her appearance of kindliness – which was, however, not exempt from a slight hint of malice – reminded me, in spite of myself, of my host's Venus. In making this comparison, which I kept to myself, I wondered whether the superior beauty that ultimately had to be conceded to the statue did not spring, to a great degree, from the fact that she had the expression of a tigress. Energy, even in evil passions, always arouses in us a certain astonishment and a kind of involuntary admiration.

"What a shame," I mused as I left Puygarrig, "that such a likeable person should be rich, and that her dowry should mean she is sought out by a man who doesn't deserve her!"

On the way back to Ille, not quite knowing what to say to Mme de Peyrehorade, but reflecting that it would only be polite to say a few words to her from time to time, I exclaimed:

"You are such freethinkers in Roussillon, Madame – holding a wedding on a Friday! In Paris, we'd be too superstitious: no man would dare to take a wife on that day."

"Good Lord, please don't talk to me about that!" she said. "If it had only been up to me, of course we'd have chosen another day. But Peyrehorade wanted it this way, and I had to give in. Still, it really bothers me. What if something dreadful happened? There must be some reason, otherwise why is everyone so frightened of Friday?"

"Friday!" cried her husband. "Friday is Venus's day!* A good day for a wedding! You see, my learned friend, I can't get my Venus out of my mind! I swear to you – it's because of her that I chose Friday. Tomorrow, if you like, before the celebration, we'll make a little sacrifice to her: we'll sacrifice two wood pigeons, and if I only knew where I could get some incense—"

"That will do, Peyrehorade!" his wife interrupted, perfectly outraged. "Burning incense to an idol! That would be an abomination! Whatever would people round here say of us?"

"At least," said M. de Peyrehorade, "you'll allow me to place a crown of roses and lilies on her head

*Manibus date lilia plenis.**

87

As you can see, Monsieur, the Constitution is a dead letter. We don't really have freedom of worship!"

The arrangements for the following day were made like this: everyone had to be all dressed up and ready at ten o'clock precisely. Once they'd drunk their chocolate, they'd go in an open carriage to Puygarrig. The civil marriage was to take place in the village *mairie*,* and the religious ceremony in the chapel of the chateau. Then would come lunch. After lunch, everyone would pass the time as they pleased until seven o'clock. At seven o'clock, they'd return to Ille, to M. de Peyrehorade's, where the two families combined would have supper together. The rest would follow naturally. Since there wouldn't be any dancing, they'd decided they'd just eat as much as possible.

At eight o'clock I was already sitting in front of Venus, a pencil in my hand, starting to draw the statue's head for the twentieth time, yet still without managing to capture its expression. M. de Peyrehorade kept coming and going round me, giving me advice, telling me over and over about his Phoenician etymologies, then he carefully placed some Bengal roses on the pedestal of the statue, and in tragicomic tones addressed to her prayers for the couple who would be living under his roof. Around nine o'clock he went in to dress for the wedding, and just then M. Alphonse appeared, squeezed into a tight new suit, with white gloves, highly polished shoes, chiselled buttons and a rose in his buttonhole.

"Will you do my wife's portrait?" he asked me, leaning over to look at my drawing. "She's pretty too!"

At that moment, on the pelota court that I have already mentioned, a game was beginning that immediately attracted M. Alphonse's attention. I in turn, tired out by my fruitless attempt to depict that diabolical face, soon left my drawing to watch the players. There were among them a few Spanish muleteers who had arrived the day before. They came from Aragon and Navarre, almost all of them wonderfully skilled players. So the locals from Ille, despite the encouragement afforded by the presence and advice of M. Alphonse, were rather quickly beaten by these new champions. The home spectators were plunged into consternation. M. Alphonse looked at his watch. It was still only half-past nine. His mother hadn't had her hair done yet. He made up his mind: he took off his formal coat, asked for a jacket and challenged the Spaniards. I watched him with a smile, somewhat surprised.

"One must stand up for the honour of one's country," he said.

At that point I found him really handsome. He was filled with passion. His elegant clothes, which had been his main preoccupation shortly before, were now forgotten. A few minutes previously, he would have been afraid to turn his head in case he got his cravat askew. *Now* he didn't spare a thought for his nicely curled hair or his carefully pleated jabot. And his fiancée?... Well, I swear that, if it had been necessary, he'd have doubtless postponed the wedding. I saw him hastily slip on a pair of sandals, roll up his sleeves and, with a confident air, set himself at the head of the vanquished party, like Caesar rallying his troops at Dyrrachium.* I jumped over the hedge, and found a comfortable spot in the shade of a nettle tree, from where I could easily see both camps.

Contrary to the general expectation, M. Alphonse missed the first ball – admittedly, it came whizzing along just above the ground, having been hit with surprising force by an Aragonese who seemed to be the leader of the Spaniards.

He was a man in his forties, wiry and muscular, six feet tall – his olive-hued skin was almost as dark-toned as the bronze of the statue of Venus.

M. Alphonse hurled his racket to the ground in a rage.

"It's this cursed ring!" he cried. "It's pinching my finger, and it's made me miss an easy ball!"

He took off his diamond ring, not without difficulty. I started to go over to take it from him, but before I could get there, he ran over to Venus, slipped his ring over her ring finger and returned to his post at the head of the Ille team.

He was pale, but calm and resolute. After this, he did not make a single mistake, and the Spanish were trounced. The enthusiasm of the spectators was a fine sight: some of them shouted repeatedly for joy and flung their hats into the air; others came to shake him by the hand, calling him "the pride of their country". If he had repelled an invasion, I doubt whether he would have received warmer and more sincere congratulations. The chagrin of the losers put the seal on his triumph.

"We'll play some more matches, old chap," he said to the Aragonese, in a tone of superiority. "But I'll give you a few points to start off with."

I'd have preferred it if M. Alphonse had been more modest, and I was almost pained at his rival's humiliation.

The Spanish giant was deeply wounded by this insult. I saw him grow pale under his suntanned skin. He gazed gloomily at his racket, tight-lipped – then, in a choked voice, he quietly said, "*Me lo pagarás.*"*

The sound of M. de Peyrehorade's voice cast a shadow over his son's triumph. My host, greatly surprised not to find him presiding over the preparations and getting the new carriage ready, was even more taken aback to see him drenched with sweat and holding a racket. M. Alphonse ran over to the house, washed his face and hands, put his new suit back on, together with his polished shoes, and five minutes later we were trotting briskly along the road to Puygarrig. All the pelota players in town and a good number of spectators followed us, uttering shouts of joy. The sturdy horses pulling us along could hardly keep ahead of those intrepid Catalans.

We had reached Puygarrig, and the procession was about to make its way on foot to the town hall, when M. Alphonse, striking his forehead, suddenly muttered to me:

"What a confounded idiot I am! I've forgotten the ring! It's on Venus's finger, damn her! Just don't tell my mother. Perhaps she won't even notice."

"You could send someone to get it," I said.

"But my servant's stayed on in Ille. Drat! I just don't trust those people. Twelve hundred francs' worth of diamonds! That might be quite a temptation for more than one of them. In any case, what an absent-minded fool people would take me for... They'd never stop laughing at me. They'd call me 'the statue's husband'. I only hope nobody steals it from me! It's a good thing the idol puts the wind up those rascals. They wouldn't dare get within an arm's length of it. Oh, who cares – I've got another ring."

The two ceremonies, civil and religious, were performed with all suitable pomp, and Mlle de Puygarrig received the ring of a little milliner from Paris without even suspecting that her fiancé was sacrificing another woman's love token to her. Then we sat down to table and started to eat, drink and even sing – and then eat, drink and sing again. I felt for the bride, who must have been put out by the vulgarity of the loud enjoyment erupting all around her – still, she put a better face on it than I could have hoped, and her embarrassment was neither clumsy and tactless, nor affected.

Perhaps, when the situation is difficult, it is possible to summon up one's courage.

When, at Heaven's behest, the lunch finally finished, it was four o'clock. The men went off to take a stroll through the grounds, which were magnificent, or else watched the peasant girls of Puygarrig, dressed in their party finery, dancing on the lawn of the chateau. In this way, we whiled away several hours. The women, however, were more eager to crowd round the bride, who was showing off the wedding presents her new husband had given her. Then she went to change, and I noticed that she had covered her lovely hair with a bonnet and a feather hat – women think first and foremost of decking themselves out, the minute they can, with all the adornments that custom forbids them to wear when they are as yet unmarried.

It was almost eight o'clock when people started to get ready to set off for Ille. But before this, a rather poignant scene took place. Mlle de Puygarrig's aunt, who had looked after her like a mother, a very elderly and deeply pious woman, would not be accompanying us back to town. Before we left, she gave her niece a touching sermon on her conjugal duties. The said sermon unleashed a flood of tears and repeated hugs and kisses. M. de Peyrehorade compared this separation to the Rape of the Sabines. Then we left, and, on our way, everyone endeavoured to distract the bride and make her laugh – but without success.

At Ille, our supper was awaiting us. And what a supper! If the vulgar enjoyment shown that morning had shocked me, I was even more shocked at the off-colour jokes and double entendres with which the bride and groom in particular were assailed. The groom, who had briefly slipped away before sitting down at table, was pale, serious and glacial in demeanour. At every moment he would take another gulp of an old Collioure wine, almost as strong as brandy.* I was sitting next to him, and felt obliged to warn him:

"Better take care, you know! They say that wine…"

I don't remember what facetious remark I made to chime in with the tone of the other guests.

He nudged my knee, and in very low tones he said:

"When we leave the table… I'd like a couple of words with you."

His solemn tone surprised me. I looked at him more attentively, and I noticed the new strangeness of his expression.

"Are you feeling a bit unwell?" I asked him.

"No."

And he started drinking again.

Meanwhile, to the accompaniment of shouts and applause, an eleven-year-old boy who had slipped under the table was showing the merrymakers a pretty white-and-pink ribbon that he had just managed to remove from the bride's ankle. They call this her "garter". It was immediately cut into pieces and distributed to the young people, who sported it in their buttonholes, in accordance with an ancient custom still observed in various patriarchal families. This caused the bride to blush to her ears… But her embarrassment knew no bounds when M. de Peyrehorade, having called for silence, sang to her a few lines of poetry in Catalan – improvised, or so he said. This is what the poem meant, if I understood correctly:

"What's going on, my friends? Is the wine I've drunk making me see double? There are two Venuses here..."

The groom suddenly looked up, with a startled expression on his face. Everyone laughed.

"Yes," continued M. de Peyrehorade, "there are two Venuses under my roof. There's the one I found in the ground, like a truffle – and then there's the other, who came down from the heavens and has just shared her girdle with us."

He meant "her garter".

"My son, choose between the two Venuses. Which do you prefer, the Roman one or the Catalan? The rascal is choosing the Catalan – a wise choice! The Roman Venus is black, the Catalan white. The Roman Venus is cold, the Catalan inflames all those who approach her!"

This cadence roused such a loud "hurrah", such noisy applause and such peals of laughter, that I thought the ceiling would fall in. All around the table, there were only three serious faces: those of the newly-weds and my own. I had a dreadful headache – and then, I don't know why, a marriage always makes me feel sad. And this one even filled me with a certain distaste.

Once the last couplets had been sung by the deputy mayor – and they were pretty racy, I have to say – we moved into the living room to enjoy the spectacle of the bride's departure. She was about to be conducted to her bedroom, since it was almost midnight.

M. Alphonse drew me into a window recess, and, looking away, said, "You'll laugh at me when I tell you... But I don't know what's wrong with me... Damn me, but I'm bewitched!"

The first idea that came into my head was that he thought himself threatened by a mishap of the kind mentioned by Montaigne and Mme de Sévigné. "The whole empire of love is filled with tragic tales",* etc.

93

"I thought this sort of accident only happened to people with a bit of imagination," I said to myself.

"You've just had a bit too much Collioure wine to drink, Monsieur Alphonse, old chap," I told him. "I *did* warn you."

"Yes, maybe. But this is something much more dreadful."

He was finding it difficult to get his words out. I thought he must be completely drunk.

"You remember my ring?" he continued after a pause.

"Yes. Has someone taken it?"

"No."

"So you've still got it?"

"No... I... I just can't get it off the finger of that diabolical Venus."

"Oh, in that case, you just haven't pulled hard enough."

"I did... But Venus... hooked her finger."

He stared at me, his face haggard, clinging to the window catch so as not to fall over.

"You're joking!" I told him. "You pushed the ring on too hard, that's all. Tomorrow you can pull it off with some pincers. But make sure you don't damage the statue."

"*No*, I'm telling you. The statue's finger moved away, curved in – she's clenching her hand, do you hear me?... She's my wife now, it appears, since I've given her my ring... She won't give it back to me."

A cold shudder suddenly ran through me, and for a moment my hair stood on end. Then he heaved a great sigh, and I caught the reek of wine on his breath, and my panic evaporated.

"The wretched man," I thought, "is completely drunk."

"You're an antiquary, Monsieur," added the groom pitifully. "You know all about those statues... perhaps there's a secret mechanism, some devilish little device that I don't know about... Would you go and have a look?"

"I'd be glad to," I said. "Come with me."

"No, I'd rather you went by yourself."

I left the living room.

The weather had changed during supper, and it was starting to pour with rain. I was about to go and ask for an umbrella when a thought stopped me. "I'd be a total idiot," I said to myself, "if I went off to check out something a drunken man has told me! Anyway, perhaps he's just trying to play some nasty trick on me, to give those honest provincials something to laugh at – and the best I can expect is to be drenched to the skin and catch a stinker of a cold."

From the door I glanced out at the statue, from which water was cascading, and I made my way up to bed without returning to the living room. I lay down, but sleep was long in coming. All the day's scenes acted themselves out in front of my mind's eye. I thought of that young woman, so beautiful and so pure, abandoned to a brutal drunkard.

"What a hateful thing an arranged marriage is!" I thought. "A mayor puts on a tricolour sash, a priest slips on a stole, and there you have it: the nicest girl in the world married to a Minotaur! Human beings who don't love each other – what can they find to say at a moment like that, a moment which two *real* lovers would pay with their lives to obtain? Can a woman ever love a man she's seen behaving coarsely even once? First impressions never fade, and I'm sure this Monsieur Alphonse will deserve the hatred he arouses…"

During my monologue, which I am here considerably abbreviating, I'd heard many comings and goings in the house, doors opening and closing, and carriages setting off; then I thought I'd heard light footfalls on the stairs, several women heading to the far end of the corridor opposite my room. This was probably the bride's procession escorting her to bed. Then they had all gone back downstairs. Mme de Peyrehorade's door had closed.

"How awkward and uncomfortable that poor girl must feel!" I said to myself. I kept twisting and turning irritably in my bed. A bachelor feels out of place and ridiculous in a house where a wedding has just been celebrated.

Silence had reigned for some time when it was broken by heavy steps climbing the staircase. The wooden stairs creaked loudly.

"What a clumsy oaf!" I exclaimed to myself. "I bet he falls downstairs!"

The noise stopped. I picked up a book to take my mind off things. It was a local statistical survey, embellished with an article by M. de Peyrehorade on the Druid monuments in the Prades district. I drowsed off at the third page.

I slept badly and woke several times. It must have been about five o'clock in the morning, and I had been awake for nearly twenty minutes, when the cock crowed. The sun was about to rise. Then I distinctly heard the same heavy steps and the same creaking stairs that I'd heard before I went to sleep. This struck me as odd. I tried, with a yawn, to imagine why M. Alphonse would be getting up so early. I couldn't think of any plausible reason. I was about to shut my eyes again when my attention was once more alerted by strange stamping noises, soon accompanied by the sound of people ringing for the servants, and the noise of doors being flung open. Then I heard a distinct hubbub of cries.

"My old drunkard must have set fire to some corner of the house!" I thought, jumping out of bed.

I got dressed hurriedly and went out into the corridor. From the opposite end, cries and lamentations could be heard, and one heart-rending voice drowned out all the others: "My son! My son!" It was obvious that some mishap had befallen M. Alphonse. I ran to the bridal bedroom – it was full of people. The first thing I caught sight of was the young man, half dressed, stretched across the bed, whose wooden frame had been broken. He was waxen-hued and motionless. His mother was weeping and wailing alongside him. M. de Peyrehorade was desperately rubbing his temples with eau de Cologne and holding smelling salts to his nose. Alas! His son had been dead for some time. On a sofa at the other side of the room lay his bride, shaken by the most horrible convulsions. She was shouting and screaming inarticulately, and two strong servant women were finding it almost impossible to restrain her.

"My God!" I cried. "Whatever's happened?"

I went over to the bed and lifted the body of the unfortunate young man: he was already stiff and cold. His clenched teeth and his blackened face expressed the most dreadful anguish. It was quite obvious that his death had been violent and his agony terrible. Yet there was no trace of blood on his clothes. I lifted his shirt and saw on his chest a livid imprint which extended right along his ribs and over onto his back. It was as if he had been embraced in the grip of some iron hoop. My foot trod on something hard on the carpet. I bent down and saw the diamond ring.

I led M. de Peyrehorade and his wife back into their room, then I had the bride carried there too.

"You still have a daughter," I told them. "You owe it to her to take care of her."

Then I left them alone.

It seemed to me beyond doubt that M. Alphonse had been the victim of an assassination. The murderers must have found some means of getting into the bride's bedroom in the middle of the night. But those bruises on the chest, and the way they circled the body, completely stumped me – a stick or an iron bar could never have produced them. Suddenly, I recalled having heard in Valence that hired thugs would sometimes use long leather bags filled with fine sand to beat to death the people they had been paid to kill. That immediately made me think of the muleteer from Aragon and his threats, but I could hardly dare to think that he would have taken such a terrible revenge for a mere light-hearted jest.

I went into the house, looking everywhere for traces of a break-in. When I found none, I went down into the garden to see if the murderers had managed to get in from there, but I didn't find any real clues. The rain of the evening before had in any case so thoroughly drenched the ground that it wouldn't have preserved any clear traces. I did, however, observe several footprints deeply imprinted in the earth: they went in two opposite directions, in parallel lines, starting from the corner of the hedge next to the pelota court and ending at the door of the house. They could have been the footprints left by M. Alphonse when he had gone looking for his ring on the statue's finger. On the other hand, the hedge at this spot was not as thick as elsewhere, so this must have been the place where the murderers got through. Walking up and down in front of the statue, I halted for a moment to look at it. This time, I must confess, I couldn't suppress a feeling of fear as I gazed at its expression of ironic malice – and, my head crowded with the horrible scenes I had just witnessed, I seemed to see an infernal deity rejoicing at the misfortune that had befallen this house.

I went back to my room and stayed there until midday. Then I went out and asked for news of my hosts. They had calmed down a little. Mlle de Puygarrig, or rather M. Alphonse's widow, had come round. She had even spoken to the public prosecutor from Perpignan, at present sitting over cases in Ille, and this magistrate had heard her statement. He asked me for mine. I told him what I knew, and did not conceal my suspicions about the Aragonese muleteer. He ordered his immediate arrest.

"Have you managed to get anything out of Madame Alphonse?" I asked the prosecutor, once my statement had been transcribed and signed.

"The unfortunate woman has gone mad," he told me with a sad smile. "Quite, quite mad! This is her story:

"She'd been in bed for a few minutes, she says, with the bed curtains closed, when the door of her room opened, and someone came in. Madame Alphonse was at that moment on the side of the bed nearest the wall, with her face turned to it. She didn't make a movement, thinking it must be her husband. A moment later, the bed creaked and groaned as if some enormous load had settled on it. She was terrified, but didn't dare look round. Five minutes, ten minutes perhaps, went by… she lost all track of time. Then she involuntarily made a movement, or the person in the bed with her did so, and she felt the touch of something as cold as ice – those are her very words. She huddled up against the wall, trembling in every limb. Shortly afterwards, the door opened a second time and someone came in, saying, 'Hello, my dear.' Shortly afterwards, the bed curtains were drawn apart. She heard a stifled cry. The person who was in bed next to her sat up, with arms held out, it seemed. Then Madame Alphonse turned round... and saw, she says, her husband on his knees at the bedside, his head level with the pillow, in the arms of a kind of greenish giant who was squeezing him in a powerful grip. She says – she's repeated it more than twenty times, poor woman! – she says that she recognized it as... would you believe it?... the bronze Venus, Monsieur de Peyrehorade's statue!... Ever since it's been around, that statue has been giving people ideas. Anyway, let me finish the story as told by the poor mad woman. At the sight of this, she lost consciousness, and she had probably already lost her mind a few minutes previously. She just cannot say how long she remained in a faint. Once she'd come back to her senses, she saw the ghost – or the statue, as she insists on saying – motionless, its legs and midriff in the bed, its upper half and arms stretching forward, and between its arms her husband, quite still. A cock crowed. Then the statue climbed out of bed, let the corpse flop down and left. Madame Alphonse pulled with all her strength on the bell for the servants. The rest you know."

They brought the Spaniard in. He was calm, and defended himself with great aplomb and presence of mind. He didn't even deny the words I'd heard him say, but he explained them away, claiming that all he'd meant was that the next day, when he was well rested, he would have won a pelota match against his so far victorious opponent. I remember that he added:

"When a man from Aragon is insulted, he doesn't wait till the next day to take his revenge. If I'd thought Monsieur Alphonse really wanted to offend me, I'd have stuck my knife in his belly that moment."

They compared his shoes with the footprints in the garden: his shoes were much bigger.

Finally the manager of the hotel where this man was staying assured us that he'd spent the night rubbing down one of his mules, which was sick.

In any case, this Aragonese was well known and highly respected in the neighbourhood, where he came on business every year. So they apologized to him and let him go.

I forgot to mention the statement made by one of the servants, the last one to see M. Alphonse alive. He had been just about to go up to his wife – he'd called this servant over and asked him anxiously if he knew where I was. The servant replied that he hadn't seen me. Then M. Alphonse heaved a sigh and stood there for a whole minute in silence, before saying: "Hang it all! The Devil must have carried him away too!"

I asked this servant if M. Alphonse was wearing his diamond ring when he spoke to him. The servant hesitated before replying – finally he said that he didn't think so... in any case, he hadn't really paid any attention.

"If he *had* been wearing the ring," he corrected himself, "I probably would have noticed it, since I thought he had given it to Madame Alphonse."

Questioning this man, I felt something of the superstitious terror that Mme Alphonse's statement had spread through the whole household. The public prosecutor gazed at me, smiling, and I decided not to take the matter any further.

A few hours after M. Alphonse's funeral, I made ready to leave Ille. M. de Peyrehorade's carriage was to take me to Perpignan. In spite of his weakened state, the poor old man insisted on accompanying me to his garden gate. We walked across it in silence; he held on to my arm, being barely able to drag himself along. As we were about to separate, I took one last look at the statue of Venus. I could imagine perfectly well that, although my host did not share the terror and hatred that she inspired among some other members of his family, he would want to get rid of an object that would forever remind him of a dreadful tragedy. My intention was to persuade him to put it in a museum. I was hesitating to broach the subject, when M. de Peyrehorade mechanically turned his head in the direction he had seen me looking in. He saw the statue, and immediately burst into tears. I embraced him and, without daring to speak a single word, climbed into the carriage.

Since my departure, nothing has emerged, as far as I've heard, to shed light on this mysterious tragedy.

M. de Peyrehorade died a few months after his son. In his will, he bequeathed his manuscripts to me. Perhaps I'll publish them one day. I never found the article about the inscriptions on the statue of Venus.

PS: My friend M. de P— has just written to me from Perpignan to say that the statue is no more. After the death of her husband, Mme de Peyrehorade wasted no time in having it melted down to make a church bell, and in this new shape it serves in the church at Ille. But, adds M. de P—, it seems that some evil spell pursues anyone who possesses this bronze. Ever since the bell has been tolling the hours in Ille, the vines have twice been ruined by frost.

Note on the Texts

I have used the texts in the excellent edition by Michael Tilby, *Prosper Mérimée: Carmen et autres nouvelles choisies* (London: George G. Harrap & Co., 1981), with its informative panoply of notes and comments. I have also drawn on Prosper Mérimée, *Théâtre de Clara Gazul; Romans et nouvelles*, ed. Jean Mallion and Pierre Salomon (Paris: Gallimard, "Bibliothèque de la Pléiade", 1978).

Notes

p. 3, *Epigraph*: "Every woman is poison [literally, "bile" or "gall" – a nuisance]. But she has two good times: one when she's in bed and the other when she's dead" (Greek). Palladas lived in Alexandria in the fifth century AD.

p. 3, *I had always suspected... all true archaeologists*: The Bastuli were a pre-Roman people who lived in the area of Spain stretching from today's Málaga in the west to Murcia in the east, and from the Mediterranean in the south to Albacete in the north. "Poeni" suggests Punic, i.e. Phoenician/Carthaginian: there were many Punic settlers from Carthage in this area, notably under Hasdrubal and Hannibal. The Battle of Munda, lasting for eight hours, was fought by Julius Caesar against Titus Labienus and the two sons of Pompey the Great on 17th March 45 BC. Caesar's devastating victory (all of the enemy standards were captured) brought the Civil War to a close. Rather curiously (see the other Mérimée story presented here, 'The Venus of Ille'), Caesar's signal for the main attack on the Pompeian army was "Venus" – he claimed to be a descendant of the goddess of love. (Aeneas, the legendary Trojan refugee ultimately responsible for the founding of Rome, was Venus's son.) A year after the battle, Caesar himself was assassinated. The site of the battle is still debated by historians. The narrator's findings on the matter were never published – one of Mérimée's semi-jocular red herrings, no doubt.

p. 3, *Caesar's Commentaries*: Probably a reference to the aforementioned *Bellum Hispaniense* ("On the Hispanic War"), no longer attributed to Julius Caesar. This account ends with the Battle of Munda.

p. 3, *the Carchena plain*: The earliest editions of the story have the name as "Cachena", and Mérimée's toponymy often differs from the standard form. (La) Carchena is about 25 km south-east of Córdoba.

p. 5, *my Elzevir edition of the Commentaries*: The Elzevir family were celebrated Dutch publishers and printers who flourished in the seventeenth and early eighteenth centuries.

p. 5, *lying on my stomach, like Gideon's bad soldiers*: Before Gideon went into battle against the Midianites, the Lord told him to reduce the number of his men: he was to keep only those who drank from a river by taking the water from their cupped hands, demonstrating that they were still on the alert (Judges 7:5–6).

p. 6, *he didn't pronounce his s in the Andalusian style*: Andalusians aspirate the *s*, and do not distinguish it in pronunciation from the soft *c* and *z*, which the Spanish pronounce like the English *th*. You can recognize an Andalusian just by the way he says "Señor" [MÉRIMÉE'S NOTE].

p. 6, *a real Havana regalia*: A Cuban high-quality cigar.

p. 6, *the partido of Montilla*: *Partido* is Spanish for "district"; Montilla is some 50 km south of Córdoba.

p. 6, *big tiles with broad rims*: This was the type of tile favoured by the Romans.

p. 6, *thirty leagues in a single day*: In the 1830s, one French league (*lieue*) was 4 km.

p. 7, *the Venta del Cuervo*: A *venta* is an inn: "Venta del Cuervo" is "The Inn of the Crow".

p. 8, *a bandit called José María*: José María Hinojosa Cabacho ("El Tempranillo", 1805–33), a bandit and something of a Robin Hood figure. He also appears in Mérimée's *Letters from Spain* (see his letter from Madrid of November 1830).

p. 8, *the description of José María… his incognito*: In his *Letters from Spain*, Mérimée writes: "José María has been described to me as a tall young man of twenty-five or thirty, well built, with a frank and laughing face, teeth as white as pearls and remarkably expressive eyes. Usually he is dressed like a village dandy, but very expensively; his shirts are dazzling white, and his hands would be a credit to any man of fashion in London or Paris." The posters set a price of 8,000 reales (that is, one thousand dollars, or piastres) for the capture of José María, dead or alive.

p. 9, *ancient Munda Baetica*: Baetica, or Hispania Baetica, was a Roman province that covered more or less the same area as today's Andalusia.

p. 9, *gazpacho, a kind of salad with peppers*: Mérimée's description is odd: gazpacho is usually a highly seasoned cold soup with tomatoes, peppers, cucumber, etc. The meal is, of course, very peppery.

p. 9, *a wineskin full of Montilla*: Montilla, currently the home of the Wine Fair of Andalusia, produces a great variety of wines, especially dessert wines.

p. 10, *zorzicos*: The *zorzico* (usual spelling *zortziko*) is a Basque folk dance. It is sometimes described as being in $\frac{5}{8}$ or $\frac{5}{4}$, but the dotted notes on the second and fourth beats give it a complex, syncopated sound. It can be heard in the unofficial Basque anthem 'Gernikako Arbola' ("The Tree of Guernica").

p. 10, *the Provinces*: The privileged provinces, enjoying particular *fueros*, i.e. Álava, Biscay, Guipúzcoa and part of Navarra. Basque is the language of this region [MÉRIMÉE'S NOTE]. *Fueros* were bodies of law, especially local or regional law.

p. 14, *alcalde*: The presiding Spanish municipal magistrate, often in effect the senior local judge.

p. 15, *you can see Diana and her nymphs bathing... Actaeon*: A reference to the Greek myth of the hunter Actaeon, who having offended Artemis (Diana) by seeing her naked was turned by her into a stag, and then killed by his own dogs.

p. 15, *the prettiest young grisette in Córdoba*: In French, a *grisette* was a lower-class young woman, pert and flirtatious, often "of easy virtue".

p. 16, *a la francesa*: "In the French style" (Spanish).

p. 16, *in the dark light that falls from the stars*: A quotation from *Le Cid* (Act IV, Sc. 3), a 1636 play by Pierre Corneille (1606–84) set in Spain.

p. 16, *papelitos*: Small cigars.

p. 16, *nevería*: A café provided with an ice box, or rather a cool place to keep snow. In Spain, practically every village has its *nevería*. [MÉRIMÉE'S NOTE]. *Nevería* is still the Spanish word for an ice-cream parlour.

p. 16, *You're English, I imagine?*: In Spain, any traveller who is not carrying samples of calico or silk with him is imagined to be English, *Inglesito*. The same is true in the Orient. In Chalcis, I had the honour to be introduced as a Μιλόρδος Φραντσέσος [MÉRIMÉE'S NOTE]. The Greek phrase is the somewhat burlesque "Milordos Frantsesos", i.e. a "French Milord".

p. 17, *Francisco Sevilla, the well-known picador*: Francisco Sevilla (1805–42) was a real-life picador in Mérimée's day.

p. 17, *your baji*: Your fortune [MÉRIMÉE'S NOTE].

p. 18, *thirty lots of sí*: Thirty "yeses", i.e. positive features.

p. 18, *See Brantôme for the rest*: Pierre de Bourdeille, seigneur de Brantôme (c.1540–1614) was a French soldier, courtier and writer. The work referred to here is his *Vies des dames galantes* ("Lives of Noble Ladies"), a collection of biographies of women with eventful love lives. The passage in question is from the book's Second Discourse, Article III: 'Of visual perception in love'.

p. 19, *Romani... gitanos*: Mérimée learnt some Romani, or *chipe calli*, while travelling in Spain in the 1830s. He was helped by his friend, the Spanish writer Serafín Estébanez Calderón (1799–1867), though the latter seems to have had a rather superficial understanding of the *gitano* culture he wrote about.

p. 20, *corregidor*: A police magistrate.

p. 21, *He's a hidalgo... so he's going to be garrotted*: In 1830, the nobility still enjoyed this privilege. Today, under the constitutional regime, commoners too have won the right to the garrotte [MÉRIMÉE'S NOTE]. Don José is a *hidalgo*. The word, from the Spanish phrase *hijo d'algo* ("son of something"), was used to refer to a member of the nobility; he was exempt from paying taxes, but could still be very poor. Don Quixote was a *hidalgo*. By Mérimée's day, the term had lost much of its upper-class sense.

p. 22, *He's in the chapel*: Prisoners awaiting execution would be detained in the prison chapel in the days preceding their death; they would be attended by a confessor.

p. 22, *"leuvely leetle execution"*: The Dominican's words are a quotation from Molière's play *Monsieur de Pourceaugnac* (Act III, Sc. 3), where they are spoken in a thickly Swiss-German-accented French – here, the quotation mainly suggests a rather smug knowingness.

p. 22, *Vittoria*: Now Vitoria-Gasteiz.

p. 23, *Elizondo, in the Baztan valley*: Elizondo is a village to the north of Pamplona.

p. 23, *an Old Christian*: The "Old Christians" of Spain and Portugal had *limpieza de sangre* ("purity of blood") – in other words their families had "always" been Christian. They were distinguished from the "New Christians" descended from Jewish or Moorish converts.

p. 23, *pelota*: Basque pelota is one of several ball games, usually played within a court, generally with rackets: the ball is flung against the wall of the court.

p. 23, *Álava*: The province of Álava has Vitoria-Gasteiz as its capital.

p. 23, *maquilas*: Sticks with steel tips [MÉRIMÉE'S NOTE].

p. 23, *the Almansa regiment*: The reference is to Almansa, a town in Albacete in the south of Spain, to which the scene now shifts. The Almansa Regiment was a noted regiment of dragoons.

p. 24, *Mr Twenty-Four*: A magistrate responsible for the police and the municipal administration [MÉRIMÉE'S NOTE].

p. 24, *blue skirts... to their shoulders*: The usual costume of peasant girls in Navarre and the Basque provinces [MÉRIMÉE'S NOTE].

p. 24, *the gitanilla*: The little *gitana*.

p. 25, *compadre*: A common form of address in Andalusia.

p. 26, *the Triana market*: Triana is a suburb of Seville, on the other side of the Guadalquivir from the main part of the city. It had a large *gitano* population.

p. 26, *Miss Carmencita... flies off her*: Carmen is being threatened with a punishment meted out in Spain at the time to alleged witches: being paraded round town on a donkey and whipped on her bare shoulders at every crossroads.

p. 26, *paint a draughts board on it*: *Pintar un javeque*, "to paint a xebec". Spanish xebecs generally have their square sails painted red and white [MÉRIMÉE'S NOTE]. A xebec was a Mediterranean sailing ship favoured by Barbary pirates.

p. 27, *the Calle Sierpes... twists and turns*: The Calle Sierpes ("Serpents' Street"), a commercial street in Seville, actually runs north-south in a very straight line: here it is deemed to be serpentine for symbolic reasons. In Spanish, *sierpe* is a formal word for a snake or serpent, but also refers to someone ugly or fierce.

p. 27, *baï, jaona*: "Yes, sir" [MÉRIMÉE'S NOTE].

p. 27, *the provinces*: That is, the Basque country.

p. 28, *Laguna*: "*Laguna*", or "*lagona*", is Basque for "friend" – Carmen uses the same word a little later. An early example of the Basque language appearing in print – possibly the first such example – is in François Rabelais's *Gargantua*, Chapter 5, where a group of partygoers are waiting for Gargantua to be born: one of the topers says "*Lagona edatera!*", Basque for "friend, let's drink!", or "drink, friend!"

p. 28, *Echalar*: Echalar, in Basque Etxalar, is a small village near Pamplona.

p. 28, *barratcea*: Enclosure, garden [MÉRIMÉE'S NOTE].

p. 28, *the white mountain*: "White mountain" is probably a reference to the Pyrenees.

p. 28, *jacques*: Bully boys, swaggerers [MÉRIMÉE'S NOTE].

p. 29, *my lance*: The entire Spanish cavalry is armed with lances [MÉRIMÉE'S NOTE].

p. 30, *Longa and Mina… poor devil like me*: The fellow Basques mentioned by Don José – Francisco de Longa (1783–1831), Francisco Espoz y Mina (1781–1836) and Joaquín Romualdo de Pablo y Antón (known as "Chapalangarra", 1784–1830) – were all prominent military leaders in the early nineteenth century. The "blacks" were Spanish liberals, as opposed to the "whites", who were royalists. Black plays a big part in 'Carmen': not least, it is the literal meaning of one of the names the Spanish *gitanos* give themselves, *calé*.

p. 30, *Alcalá*: Alcalá de los Panaderos, a small town two leagues from Seville, where they make delicious small loaves. They claim that they derive their excellent quality from the water in Alcalá, and every day they bring a great number of them into Seville [MÉRIMÉE'S NOTE]. Alcalá de Guadaíra is commonly known as Alcalá de los Panaderos, "Alcalá of the Breadmakers", as its many bakers supplied most of Seville's bread.

p. 30, *two-piastre*: A piastre was equivalent to a Spanish dollar.

p. 31, *a tambourine*: In French, this is a *tambour de basque* – something else to make Don José feel homesick.

p. 32, *"Agur laguna"*: "Hello there, friend" [MÉRIMÉE'S NOTE].

p. 32, *I could see… the bars of the gate*: Most houses in Seville have an inner court surrounded by porticoes. This is where people gather in summer. This court is covered by a canvas that is kept watered during the day and is pulled in at night. The front door is almost always covered, and the passage that leads to the court, *zaguán*, is closed off by an iron gate of most elegant workmanship [MÉRIMÉE'S NOTE].

p. 33, *Tomorrow's another day, eh?*: Mañana será otro día – Spanish proverb [MÉRIMÉE'S NOTE].

p. 33, *A dog on the prowl will soon find a fowl*: Chuquel sos pirela, / Cocal terela. "A dog who walks, a bone does find" – Romani proverb [MÉRIMÉE'S NOTE].

p. 33, *yemas*: Sugared egg yokes [MÉRIMÉE'S NOTE].

p. 33, *turrón*: A kind of nougat [MÉRIMÉE'S NOTE].

p. 33, *King Don Pedro the Just*: King Don Pedro, whom we call "the Cruel" in French and whom the Catholic Queen Isabella never called anything other than "the Just", liked to stroll through the streets of Seville in the evening, seeking adventures, like the Caliph Harun al-Rashid. One night, in an isolated backstreet, he picked a quarrel with a man who was serenading. They fought, and the king killed the amorous knight. At the sound of the swords clashing, an old woman looked out of the window, and lit up the scene with the little lamp, *candilejo*, that she was holding. You need to know that the King Don Pedro, who in other respects was agile and vigorous, had one strange physical defect: whenever he walked, his knee joints would make a loud creaking sound. The old woman had no difficulty recognizing him from this creaking. The next day, the sergeant on duty came to make his report to the king.

"Sire, there was a duel fought last night, in such and such a street. One of the combatants was killed."

"Have you found out who the murderer was?"

"Yes, sire."

"Why has he not already been punished?"

"Sire, I await your orders."

"Execute the law."

Now, the king had just published a decree announcing that any duellist would be decapitated, and his head exposed over the place of combat. The sergeant found an ingenious way out of his predicament. He ordered the head of one of the statues of the king to be sawn off, and exposed it in a niche halfway down the street that had been the scene of the murder. The king and all the inhabitants of Seville found this a very good solution. The street took its name from the lamp of the old woman who had been the sole witness to the affair. That at least is the folk tradition. Zúñiga tells the story slightly differently (see *Annales de Sevilla,* Book II, p. 136). Whatever the truth of the matter, there is still in Seville a Street of the Candilejo, and in this street a stone bust which is said to be the portrait of Don Pedro. Unfortunately, this bust is modern. The old one was already quite eroded in the seventeenth century, and the municipality of the day had it replaced by the one you can see today [MÉRIMÉE'S NOTE]. The original bust can now be seen in the Casa de Pilatos in Seville. Peter of Castile (called "the Just" or "the Cruel", 1334–69) was King of Castile and León from 1350 to 1359. Harun al-Rashid (763–809), immortalized in *The Arabian Nights,* was the fifth Abbasid Caliph of Baghdad. The Spanish historian Diego Ortiz de Zúñiga (1636–80) was the author of the monumental *Annales eclesiásticos y seculares de la muy noble y muy leal ciudad de Sevilla* (Madrid: Imprenta Real, 1677) a historical account of the events in Seville from 1246 to 1671 (the story of King Don Pedro's dangerous scrape in the Calle Candilejo is actually told in Book VI, pp. 210–11).

p. 34, *rom... romi*: *Rom*, "husband"; *romi*, "wife" [MÉRIMÉE'S NOTE].

p. 34, *Calé*: Calo; feminine: *calli*; plural: *calé*. Literally, "black" – the name the *gitanos* give themselves in their language [MÉRIMÉE'S NOTE].

p. 35, *You're a real canary... character*: Spanish dragoons wear yellow uniforms [MÉRIMÉE'S NOTE].

p. 35, *the law of Egypt*: That is, the law of the *gitanos*, who were often imagined to have come from Egypt.

p. 35, *I may be dressed in wool, but I'm no sheep: Me dicas vriardâ de jorpoy, bus ne sino braco* – Romani proverb [MÉRIMÉE'S NOTE].

p. 35, *majari*: Saint; the Blessed Virgin [MÉRIMÉE'S NOTE].

p. 35, *a certain old widow with a wooden leg*: The gibbet, which is the wife of the last man hanged there [MÉRIMÉE'S NOTE].

p. 35, *Laloro*: The Red (land) [MÉRIMÉE'S NOTE].

p. 36, *old chum*: Here and elsewhere, Carmen addresses Don José (in the French text) as *mon pays*, meaning a compatriot or man from the same part of the world. (*Le pays* can also simply mean "country" or "homeland".) She thus maintains the pretence (if it is one) of being a fellow Basque.

p. 36, *duro*: A Spanish dollar, or piastre, equivalent to eight reales.

p. 39, *a Flemish Romani lass*: *Flamenca de Roma* – a slang term for *gitana*. Roma does not here mean the Eternal City, but the nation of Romi or married people, the name the *gitanos* give themselves. The first *gitanos* to be seen in Spain probably came from the Low Countries, hence their being called "Flemish" [MÉRIMÉE'S NOTE].

p. 39, *chufas*: A bulbous root from which quite a pleasant drink is made [MÉRIMÉE'S NOTE].

p. 39, *rice or hake*: The ordinary food of the Spanish soldier [MÉRIMÉE'S NOTE].

p. 39, *steal à pastesas*: *Ustilar à pastesas*, to steal skilfully, to rob without violence [MÉRIMÉE'S NOTE]. Literally, to steal "with the hands" or "by any sleight of hand".

p. 39, *miñones*: A kind of militia unit [MÉRIMÉE'S NOTE].

p. 40, *El Dancaire*: The nickname "Dancaire" denotes a man who gambles for other people, using their money.

p. 40, *Gaucín*: Gaucín, like the fishing town of Estepona a few lines down, is near Gibraltar.

p. 41, *the scabs that give you pleasure do not itch*: Sarapia sat pesquital ne punzava [MÉRIMÉE'S NOTE] (Spanish Romani).

p. 41, *Vejer*: Vejer de la Frontera is a hilltop town overlooking the Straits of Gibraltar.

p. 41, *in the presidio at Tarifa*: That is, in jail in Tarifa, on the Straits of Gibraltar.

p. 42, *Écija... El Remendado*: Écija is a town east of Seville; "Remendado" literally means "patched together", and thus "ragged", "tattered".

p. 44, *The lillipendi think I'm an erani*: "The idiots take me for a respectable lady" [MÉRIMÉE'S NOTE].

p. 45, *the Lobsters*: Name given by the lower classes in Spain to the English because of the colour of their uniform [MÉRIMÉE'S NOTE].

p. 45, *Rollona*: The name Rollona suggests "plump" (or "a bore").

p. 45, *to finibus terræ*: To the galleys, or to hell [MÉRIMÉE'S NOTE]. The cod-Latin phrase suggests "the ends of the earth".

p. 47, *my minchorrò*: "My lover", or, rather, "my whim" [MÉRIMÉE'S NOTE].

p. 47, *Maquila... is an orange*: See fifth note to p. 23.

p. 48, *crocodile laughs*: Both French and Spanish have phrases for "crocodile tears" – *larmes de crocodile, lágrimas de cocodrilo*.

p. 49, *a true Navarrese*: Navarro fino [MÉRIMÉE'S NOTE].

p. 49, *the dwarf... can spit a long way*: Or esorjié de or narsi-chislé, sin chismar lachinguel – a Romani proverb. The prowess of a dwarf is that he can spit a long way [MÉRIMÉE'S NOTE].

p. 51, *a lillipendi*: See note to p. 44.

p. 53, *Zacatín*: The commercial district of Granada at that time.

p. 53, *A river that makes a noise… pebbles in it*: *Len sos sonsi abela / Pani o reblendani terela* – a Romani proverb [MÉRIMÉE'S NOTE].

p. 54, *the bull's cockade*: *La divisa*, a bow of ribbons whose colour indicates the pasture the bulls come from. This bow is stuck into the animal's skin by means of a hook, and it is a mark of supreme gallantry to tear it away from the living animal and offer it to a woman [MÉRIMÉE'S NOTE].

p. 56, *María Padilla… the Great Queen of the gitanos*: María Padilla was accused of having put a spell on King Don Pedro. One folk tradition recounts that she had presented Queen Blanche of Bourbon with a golden belt, which appeared to the king's spell-bound eyes to have the shape of a living serpent. Hence the repugnance he always showed for the unhappy princess. [MÉRIMÉE'S NOTE]. The Castilian noblewoman María de Padilla (*c.*1334–61) was King Don Pedro's long-time mistress. King Don Pedro (see fifth note to p. 33) married, under coercion from his family, the fourteen-year-old Blanche of Bourbon (1339–61) in 1353.

p. 58, *It's the fault… like that*: This is where Don José's narrative ends. What follows is Mérimée's short essay on *gitanos*, based largely on George Borrow.

p. 59, *the name of Calé… refer to themselves*: I have noticed that the German Roma, although they understand the word *Calé* perfectly well, did not like being given that name. They call each other *Romané tchavé* [MÉRIMÉE'S NOTE].

p. 59, *like Panurge… in the neck*: Panurge is an ebullient but at times cowardly trickster in Rabelais (see, in particular, *Pantagruel*, Chapter 21).

p. 60, *Casta quem nemo rogavit*: "She's chaste because no one has ever asked her" (Ovid, *Amores* I, 8).

p. 62, *campo santo*: A *campo santo* is a graveyard or cemetery.

p. 64, *The Mysteries of Paris*: *The Mysteries of Paris* (1842–43) was a best-selling novel by Eugène Sue (1804–57) about low life in Paris. It deploys a great range of *argot*.

p. 64, *Monsieur Vidocq*: Eugène-François Vidocq (1775–1857) was a French criminal who eventually became Chief of Police.

p. 65, *Oudin, in his curious dictionary (1640)*: A reference to *Curiosités françaises pour servir de supplément aux dictionnaires* ("French curiosities serving as a supplement to dictionaries") by the French lexicographer Antoine Oudin (1595–1653).

p. 65, *But an etymology... genius of his language*: It has been observed that Mérimée's etymology of the word *frimousse* is confected – one of his little jokes.

p. 69, *Epigraph*: "'Let this statue,' I said, 'be gracious and beneficent, so closely does it resemble a man.'" From *Philopseudes* ("The Lover of Lies") by Lucian of Samosata (2nd century AD).

p. 69, *Canigou... Ille*: The Canigou is the highest mountain in the Pyrénées-Orientales; Ille-sur-la-Têt (now more often Ille-sur-Têt) is a small town in Catalonia, between Perpignan and Prades.

p. 70, *Serrabone*: Serrabone (in Catalan, Serrabona) is the location of a priory in the Pyrénées-Orientales which Merimée had visited.

p. 71, *Louis-Philippe*: Louis-Philippe (1773–1850) was the "Citizen King" of France from 1830 to 1848.

p. 73, *miliasses*: Cakes made from maize flour.

p. 73, *Journal des modes*: *Le Journal des dames et des modes* was a French fashion magazine published between 1797 and 1839.

p. 75, *sancta simplicitas*: "Blessed naivety" (Latin).

p. 75, *Tuileries... Coustou's insipid figures*: A reference to the French sculptor Nicolas Cousteau (1658–1733). His statues are in the Tuileries Garden in Paris.

p. 75, *My housewife... due reverence*: A parody of some lines (Act I, Sc. 2) in *Amphitryon*, a 1668 comedy by Molière (1622–73).

p. 75, *Myro*: A Greek sculptor of the fifth century BC.

p. 76, *Veneris nec præmia noris*: "You will not know the gifts of Venus" (Virgil, *Aeneid* IV, 33). In the original context, it is a question – here it acts as a sly reference to venereal disease.

p. 77, *Montagnes régalades*: Roughly, "kingly mountains". 'Muntanyes Regalades' is a medieval Catalan song.

p. 79, *"Morra Player"… morra*: Morra is an Italian game for two players, in which each of them throws out one to five fingers and simultaneously calls a number between two and ten, trying to guess how many fingers will be held up in total. The so-called "Germanicus", a Roman statue in the Louvre, appears to be making a morra gesture with his right hand.

p. 80, *It is Venus… her prey!*: A quotation from *Phèdre* (Act I, Sc. 3, l. 306), a 1677 tragedy by Racine (1639–99), suggesting the overwhelming might of the Goddess of Love, who has forced Phaedra to fall in love with her stepson Hippolytus.

p. 80, *"Quid dicis, doctissime?"*: "What do you say to that, my most learned friend?" (Latin).

p. 81, *specs*: The narrator uses an archaic word for "spectacles" found in Rabelais, namely *besicles* – in *Gargantua* (Chapter I), the narrator needs a "grand reinforcement of spectickles" to make out an enigmatic text.

p. 82, *Eutyches Myro*: It has been pointed out that the name "Eutyches" means, among other things, "fortunate" or "prosperous"; followed by "Myro", this gives – with a little imagination – "Prosper Mérimée".

p. 83, *Boulternère was a Phoenician town!*: Mérimée is here indulging in playful etymological fantasy, as in his linguistic essay at the end of 'Carmen': the name "Boulternère" is derived from the name of the local river, the Boulès, followed by *ternera*, a Catalan contraction of *terra negra* ("black earth" – rich and easy to cultivate).

p. 83, *Tetricus… the town of Turbul*: Tetricus I and his son Tetricus II were co-rulers of the short-lived breakaway Gallic Empire which was separated from the Roman Empire between

260 and 274 AD. The information about Nera Pivesuvia and the two Tetricuses was probably taken by Mérimée from *Mémoire sur quelques monumens inédits représentant Claude le Gothique, Nera Pivesuvia et les deux Tetricus* (1834) by the French scholar and archaeologist Alexandre Du Mège (1780–1862).

p. 84, *Gruter... or Orelli*: Jan Gruter (1560–1627) was a Flemish-born philologist; Johan Caspar von Orelli (1787–1849) was a Swiss scholar. They both produced compendious catalogues of epigraphs.

p. 85, *Diomedes... white birds*: In Homer, the Greek hero Diomedes wounded Venus at the siege of Troy (*Iliad* v). Later legends had Venus taking her revenge by changing his companions into white birds (see, for example, Ovid's *Metamorphoses* XIV, ll. 496 ff.).

p. 87, *Venus's day*: In French: *vendredi*, "day of Venus".

p. 87, *Manibus date lilia plenis*: "Strew great handfuls of lilies" (Virgil, *Aeneid* VI, l. 883). In its original context, there is a mournful note to these words: they occur during Aeneas's descent into the underworld; the shade of his father Anchises utters them to pay homage to the shade of Marcellus (42–23 BC), the nephew of Emperor Augustus. Marcellus might have inherited the position of emperor, but died prematurely – not an irrelevant allusion in Mérimée's story.

p. 88, *mairie*: "Town hall" (French).

p. 89, *Dyrrachium*: The site of a battle (in Illyria) where Julius Caesar was defeated by Pompey in 48 BC.

p. 90, *"Me lo pagarás"*: "I'll make you pay for this" (Spanish).

p. 92, *an old Collioure wine, almost as strong as brandy*: Collioure, in the Roussillon region, is usually thought of as producing rather dry table wines.

p. 93, *Montaigne and Mme de Sévigné tragic tales*: Both Michel de Montaigne (1533–92) and Mme de Sévigné (1626–95) mention temporary impotence. The quotation is from Mme de Sévigné's letter to Mme de Grignan of 8th April 1671.

EVERGREENS SERIES

Beautifully produced classics, affordably priced

Alma Classics is committed to making available a wide range of literature from around the globe. Most of the titles are enriched by an extensive critical apparatus, notes and extra reading material, as well as a selection of photographs. The texts are based on the most authoritative editions and edited using a fresh, accessible editorial approach. With an emphasis on production, editorial and typographical values, Alma Classics aspires to revitalize the whole experience of reading classics.

For our complete list and latest offers

visit

almabooks.com/evergreens

101-PAGE CLASSICS
Great Rediscovered Classics

This series has been created with the aim to redefine and enrich the classics canon by promoting unjustly neglected works of enduring significance. These works, beautifully produced and mostly in translation, will intrigue and inspire the literary connoisseur and the general reader alike.

THE PERFECT COLLECTION OF LESSER-KNOWN WORKS BY MAJOR AUTHORS

almabooks.com/101-pages

GREAT POETS SERIES

Each volume is based on the most authoritative text, and reflects Alma's commitment to provide affordable editions with valuable insight into the great poets' works.

Selected Poems
Blake, William
ISBN: 9781847498212
£7.99 • PB • 288 pp

The Rime of the Ancient Mariner
Coleridge, Samuel Taylor
ISBN: 9781847497529
£7.99 • PB • 256 pp

Complete Poems
Keats, John
ISBN: 9781847497567
£9.99 • PB • 520 pp

Paradise Lost
Milton, John
ISBN: 9781847498038
£7.99 • PB • 320 pp

Sonnets
Shakespeare, William
ISBN: 9781847496089
£4.99 • PB • 256 pp

Leaves of Grass
Whitman, Walt
ISBN: 9781847497550
£8.99 • PB • 288 pp

MORE POETRY TITLES

Dante Alighieri: *Inferno, Purgatory, Paradise, Rime, Vita Nuova, Love Poems*; Alexander Pushkin: *Lyrics Vol. 1 and 2, Love Poems, Ruslan and Lyudmila*; François Villon: *The Testament and Other Poems*; Cecco Angiolieri: *Sonnets*; Guido Cavalcanti: *Complete Poems*; Emily Brontë: *Poems from the Moor*; Anonymous: *Beowulf*; Ugo Foscolo: *Sepulchres*; W.B. Yeats: *Selected Poems*; Charles Baudelaire: *The Flowers of Evil*; Sándor Márai: *The Withering World*; Antonia Pozzi: *Poems*; Giuseppe Gioacchino Belli: *Sonnets*; Dickens: *Poems*

WWW.ALMABOOKS.COM/POETRY

ALMA CLASSICS

ALMA CLASSICS aims to publish mainstream and lesser-known European classics in an innovative and striking way, while employing the highest editorial and production standards. By way of a unique approach the range offers much more, both visually and textually, than readers have come to expect from contemporary classics publishing.

LATEST TITLES PUBLISHED BY ALMA CLASSICS

www.almaclassics.com